The Man Who Told the Truth

Other books by Loula Grace Erdman

THE YEARS OF THE LOCUST

LONELY PASSAGE

THE EDGE OF TIME

THREE AT THE WEDDING

THE FAR JOURNEY

THE SHORT SUMMER

MANY A VOYAGE

THE WIND BLOWS FREE

THE WIDE HORIZON

THE GOOD LAND

The Man Who Told the Truth

WITH SIX SHORT STORIES

Loula Grace Erdman

DODD, MEAD & COMPANY
NEW YORK

L. M.
March 21-62.
030

THE MAN WHO TOLD THE TRUTH and THE HALFWAY TREE, Copyright ©
1961 by Loula Grace Erdman. Reprinted by permission of *Redbook Maga-
zine*, McCall Corporation. THE VOYAGER, Copyright 1950 by Christian
Herald Magazine. THANKS TO AUNT MILLICENT, Copyright 1947 by Loula
Grace Erdman. Reprinted by permission of *Woman's Day Magazine*, a
Fawcett publication. THE NEW HOUSE, Copyright 1952 by Loula Grace
Erdman. Reprinted by permission of *Woman's Home Companion*, The
Crowell-Collier Publishing Company. THE BOY IN THE BACK SEAT, © 1955
The Curtis Publishing Company. BONUS OF HAPPINESS, Copyright 1952 by
Loula Grace Erdman. Reprinted by permission of *Redbook Magazine*,
McCall Corporation.

Transfer
from ✗
3-16-70

Library of Congress Catalog Card Number: 62-8210
Printed in the United States of America
by Vail-Ballou Press, Inc., Binghamton, N.Y.

E 66ma

To Lilian Kastendyke

with admiration and appreciation

Contents

The Man Who Told the Truth

The Man Who Told the Truth

- 1 -

HE GOT OFF THE EIGHT THIRTY SOUTHBOUND BUS ONE MORN-
ing in late August. Although Benson was a rest stop, he
did not join the other passengers in their rush to Martin's
Café. Instead, he walked to the door of the bus station and
stood looking out at the small Texas town webbing out
from the courthouse square. Gradually his look of uncertainty gave way to one of purpose and decision. The other
passengers were boarding the bus when he shook himself
slightly—after the manner of a man whose mind is made
up—and went to the driver to request that his bag be re-
trieved from the luggage compartment. This done, he
walked out into the street, mingling with the townspeople
on their way to work.

1

The Man Who Told the Truth

Aside from the fact that he carried a suitcase, there was nothing to set him apart from the others. He was on the tall side, but not noticeably so. His clothes were neither shabby nor particularly good. In no way did he call attention to himself. But even so, the people of Benson noticed him and knew him for a stranger.

Miss Stacie Sheperd saw him as she unlocked the front door of her library. That's what everyone called it—Miss Stacie's library—although actually it belonged to the town. She mentioned him later when she telephoned her good friend Bess Dawson, who was chairbound by arthritis and sat all day with her telephone at her elbow. Miss Stacie was Bess Dawson's eyes and ears, her peephole on the world. Between them, they knew everything that went on in the town.

Shelley Carew saw the stranger too, as she paused momentarily at the door of the bank. Though she had braced herself for the workday ahead and fixed her attention on matters of business, actually she wanted nothing more than to crawl off by herself and whimper like a hurt animal, indulging herself in thoughts of past events that for months she had made an effort to forget.

From his office on the east side of the town square Dr. Larry Beckwith gave the stranger only a fleeting glance, being more concerned with watching Shelley Carew standing at the door of the bank. His heart twisted briefly as he saw how small and vulnerable she looked. He half rose from his seat with the impulsive idea of running out to her and calling, "Shelley, I didn't mean it. Or if I did, I'm sorry now." But even as he made the gesture, he saw that she had squared her shoulders, lifted her head and put on that old familiar air of self-sufficiency. Then she walked inside the bank, out of his sight.

Ben Langley, standing at the front door of his dry goods store, saw the stranger too, his practiced eye noting that the man needed a new suit and shoes. But, Ben reflected moodily, even in the unlikely event the man came in to purchase these items—passengers almost never bought anything more than handkerchiefs—Max Butler, who had spent his summer vacation helping in the men's department, would ruin the sale. Much as Ben needed help, he was glad college would start next week and Max would be off to Austin. If he could only get himself some responsible help, he thought—knowledgeable and dependable and willing to learn—he and Hallie could vacation in Florida for a couple of months. After Christmas and inventory, of course.

Martha Donnell, on her way to take her young nephew to Dr. Beckwith for his preschool shots, was the first person the stranger spoke to. He stopped her and asked politely, "Excuse me, but could you tell me if there is a good hotel in town?"

She liked his voice. It was deep, more soft than harsh, with undertones of the South overlaid with Middle West. There was no way of telling where he had come from, just as there was no way of judging his age—mid-thirties, maybe a little younger. His dark hair had a few threads of gray at the temples. There were squint lines at the corners of his dark eyes and long lines bracketing his mouth. An interesting face, Martha thought, without being either ugly or handsome—it was in between, like his age and his way of speaking.

"I'm sorry," she told him, feeling her nephew crowd close to her. "Our one hotel closed some time ago. There's a good motel, though, and there's Mrs. Higdon's."

"Does she serve meals?"

"The best," Martha said.

"Thank you," he said. "What is her address?"

Martha smiled involuntarily. No one thought in terms of addresses in Benson.

"Two blocks east and then turn to your right," she told him, gesturing. "It's that two-story yellow frame house —the one just back of the big brick one."

Almost everyone in Benson used the Thorndyke house to orient themselves and newcomers to the town.

"Thank you," he said. He gave her a curious little salute, dignified yet friendly, and walked off in the direction of Daisy Higdon's.

4

The Man Who Told the Truth

Ursula Thorndyke saw him as he walked up the steps of Mrs. Higdon's roominghouse. She had got to the kitchen by holding onto chairs as she walked. Maybe if she drank some coffee this awful feeling in her head would go away—just for a little while; she wouldn't ask for the impossible and expect it to leave her for a full day. For a moment she regarded the chrome coffeemaker, thinking real coffee might help more, but discarded the idea as being too much trouble. Instead, she measured out two teaspoons of instant coffee, her hands shaking so much that she decided to use hot water from the tap rather than risk trying to manage a kettle of boiling water.

After a few sips of coffee she felt a little better. She looked across the yard and saw that the stranger had gone inside Daisy Higdon's house. Probably a new roomer, she thought.

Like everyone else who had seen him, Ursula wondered about him—what he was doing there, why he had come in the first place and how long he would stay. But, she reasoned, if he stayed for any length of time, they'd all find out about him. Benson was like that—no one in town was allowed even the shred of a secret. She should be used to it by now, but it still bothered her.

Dr. Larry Beckwith replaced the phone on its cradle. He had just finished telling Bess Dawson that about all she could do for her pain was to take aspirin, but if she wanted him to drop by he'd come. And she had said, My goodness, no, she couldn't afford to pay him just to sit and gab, if he weren't going to do anything for her. She had listened to him free for too many years to throw away good money on him now.

Larry grinned wryly and reflected on the peculiar problem of practicing medicine in one's home town. He had nothing to complain about in the size of his practice, especially considering that he was little more than a year past his internship and had not been able to afford to do a residency. But these days patients demanded specialists. Once in medical school he had remarked ruefully that anyone having a pain in the left ear wanted a left-ear specialist, or if the pain was in the lobe, a specialist who concentrated on left lobes. But that, his roommate had reminded him sensibly, was probably sour grapes on his part. He was willing to concede the point but he had never quite relinquished the thought.

His difficulty in Benson was not lack of practice, or even a demand by his patients that he have more training. It was, quite logically, that people remembered him with more reason and greater clarity as the boy who had once delivered their papers, brought their orders from Langley's store and run their errands.

He drummed his fingers idly on the desk he had inherited along with old Dr. Grayson's office. Early as it was, there were already several patients waiting in the outer office. Miss Williams (also inherited)—who acted as his nurse, secretary and office manager—had registered them in order of their arrival. She believed firmly that it was unwise for patients to be admitted as soon as they came in. Such undignified haste, she thought, would cause people to assume that the doctor did not have a large practice, and would therefore weaken their faith in him. Had the matter been left to Larry, he would have roamed out into the waiting room himself, saying hello to all his friends, both young and old, and asking, "Who's next?" thus leaving the matter of their entrance to their own sense of fair play. However Larry found it easier to bow to Nurse Williams' experience in this and so he stayed in the inner office, seated behind the desk. Sometimes he wondered—briefly, and never without smiling a little to himself—if the patients did not draw just as much comfort from the sight of Dr. Grayson's old desk and memories of the past as they did from his own prescriptions. Larry never discounted the part a patient's own mind and feelings had in healing.

And if he knew so blasted much about what went on in people's minds, he asked himself scornfully, why hadn't he been able to work out things better between himself and Shelley Carew?

7

Now, when it was too late, he admitted that he couldn't honestly remember when he had fallen in love with her. Nor could he remember a time when he hadn't known her—a leggy, slant-eyed child who lived in the big house down the block from his own family's cottage.

Jim Carew, Shelley's father, had counted his ranch in sections, not acres, and hadn't quite known himself exactly how many they added up to. His great weakness was his cattle—the Carew herds were regarded with respect and envy all over the state. He loved good horses too, and rode them. But though he kept a Cadillac in the garage, he usually drove a smaller car himself, bumping about the ranch, not always using the roads that crisscrossed it.

He kept a keen eye on the town and its needs and was usually the first person—often the only one—to help in bringing some necessary improvement. Everybody knew that without his check the first of each month Miss Stacie would have to close the library, just as they knew that he had contributed not only the site on which the Community Hall was built, but much of the cash as well. There was not a church in town that had not benefited from his contributions—he made no distinction among the denominations—and every school child knew he was the person to approach when new band uniforms or other equipment was needed. On the rare occasions when someone—usually a visitor—remarked that Jim Carew acted as if he owned the town, the residents of Benson said he spent enough money on it to enjoy the right to act in any way he pleased. Without Jim Carew the town wouldn't even have a bank, for he had not only been one of the founders but also the chief stockholder since the day it was established. Nobody got very far criticizing Jim Carew in Benson.

He had a genuine interest in the town and its welfare, but the joy of his life—his delight, his treasure—was his daughter Shelley.

People said that the Carews might as well have adopted the girl, what with the faintly foreign look of her slanty green eyes and olive skin and black hair. Dr. Grayson, who had delivered her properly enough in the Carew house, said she was a throwback to some Black Irish ancestor for such things did happen, but that she'd grow up to be like her parents—well, he amended his statement, almost like them. But she never did, although she inherited her father's disposition—independent, stubborn, strong-willed, and never caring what anyone thought. People explained that when a couple waited as long as the Carews had for their first baby, they could expect a changeling child.

Larry Beckwith was thirteen to Shelley Carew's eight when she began to follow him around. "Wait a minute, Larry," she'd call down the length of the block. "Wait a minute! I'm coming!"

She would race toward him, her long, thin, jean-clad

9

legs flashing down the walk, black pigtails flying out behind her. Once she caught up with him, she'd act as his shadow while he delivered his papers or made collections—chattering, chattering, chattering. He told himself he didn't hear a word she said, but once or twice—when she had a cold and her mother wouldn't let her out or she was off with her family on a trip—he found his rounds oddly lonely. At such times he admitted, if only to himself, that maybe he had got used to her and even liked having her tag after him.

When he was fifteen he got his driver's license and began making deliveries for Mr. Langley in the store truck after school and on Saturdays. More often than not, Shelley hailed him at his first stop and made the rounds with him. By now she wore her hair in a ponytail, had grown a couple of inches and was as thin as a slat. But in one way she hadn't changed; she could still talk his arm off.

"You know what?" she had asked him one day, tilting her head to one side. "Your hair is the color of straw."

"So what?" he said unconcernedly.

"But it is," she went on. "Like wheat stubble, just after the wheat's been cut."

He took a quick look at himself in the rear-view mirror and decided she was right. Texas sun could bleach out a fellow's hair until it did look like straw.

The right to criticize his appearance was, however, a privilege she reserved for herself. One day he came upon her, jeans dirty and torn, her hair hanging loose about her face, a long scratch across her upper lip.

"Good Lord, Shelley, what happened?" he asked.

"I had a fight with a girl," she told him.

"Look here, brat—girls don't fight," he said.

"I had to fight her," Shelley went on, "because . . ." She paused—not out of any feeling of guilt, he was sure, but out of reluctance to reveal the cause. "She said you were ugly."

"Oh." He realized tact demanded he refrain from laughing. "I am, you know," he told her kindly.

She regarded him intently. Already the cut lip was swelling, but she was losing the wild look in her eyes.

"Well, you're not so *very* ugly," she said. "And besides, I like the way you look."

"Thank you," he told her, feeling the occasion called for some gratitude on his part. "Now you'd better go home and tell your mother what you did. The other girl's mother has probably already phoned her, and it's always best to tell on yourself. Remember that."

She stood, considering his words a moment before she turned to go. Then she stopped and looked over her shoulder. "I can't tell her," she said. "She's having one of her spells, and your mother's with her."

She made the announcement with the unashamed candor of a child who has long since learned to accept a fact of her own life at home. "Would it be all right if I told Daddy instead?" she asked.

"Oh, sure—sure," he told her, feeling awkward and beyond his depth.

"I know what *he'll* say," she went on. "He'll tell me that it was all right for me to stick up for a friend."

And that, substantially, was what Jim Carew did say, as Larry's mother told him later when she came home to report the matter. Nellie Carew was feeling better, she said, without going into the details so familiar to everyone in town. It was "poor Mrs. Carew's" age that was working on her; she was having an awful time. . . .

Once or twice it occurred to Larry that the Carews might not like the idea of having their daughter tagging around after a boy on his paper route or riding with him in a delivery truck. He knew for a fact—Shelley had told him—that Mrs. Carew had complained to her husband, saying that it made Shelley look even more like a tomboy than she was, and goodness knew it was bad enough as things stood. But Jim Carew had laughed, according to Shelley's version of the story, and said Larry Beckwith was a nice boy and would look after her and it was better for her to be out in the fresh air than sitting inside reading or doing fancy-work. Anyway, anything Baby (he called her that till the day he died) wanted to do was okay with him.

And that, Larry thought now, explained Shelley Carew in one sentence. Whatever she wanted, her father had got for her. Well, not everything; for she had wanted him, Larry Beckwith—or had said she did—and her father hadn't got him for her.

She had first put the wish into words the summer when he came home after two years in the Navy, still wearing his uniform because his civilian clothes no longer fitted. His plan was to enroll at Austin in the fall, using the GI Bill as far as it would stretch and supplementing it by working on the side. He was going to be a doctor.

He was standing in front of Ben Langley's store, considering how he could best invest his clothes budget, when he became aware of a girl coming toward him. She was wearing a sleeveless green dress with a matching sweater over her shoulders, and she walked lightly, like a bird skimming along.

Then he heard her say, "My goodness, Larry, don't you know me?"

It was Shelley Carew, grown up. No wonder he didn't know her. She was still slender, but rounded out in the right places, and she wore her hair in a shoulder-length bob instead of the ponytail he remembered. The slanting eyes were the same, and her slightly husky voice, and as always, he found they had the power to move him.

"Don't you want to buy me a Coke?" she asked.

He followed her into the drugstore.

"I can't get over it," he marveled when they were seated at a table. "I turned my back on you and you grew up."

"High time I did," she said. "I'm sixteen—well, almost."

"I'd say you weren't a day under seventeen," he told her, and she smiled easily, without the self-consciousness of so many girls her age. That, of course, could come from the way she had lived—traveling everywhere with her parents, shopping at Neiman-Marcus as casually as other girls went to Ben Langley's.

"What have you been doing with yourself?" he asked. "Besides growing up, of course."

"Oh," she said carelessly, "we took a trip last year." The Carews had gone to Europe, he found out later.

"And this past year I've been in school," she added. She had gone to a girls' school in Virginia and hated it, he eventually learned.

"And back to school this fall?" he asked.

"Yes—to high school here at home."

So she still called Benson "home." That was her father's influence.

"And you?" she asked.

"I'm going to the university," he told her. Suddenly it seemed very important that he tell her. "I'm going to try to make a doctor out of myself."

"Good," she said, leaning across the table to look straight at him, her almond-shaped eyes candid and sure. "Good. And when you're finished you can come back home to Benson and marry me."

He felt himself growing red; even his ears were fiery. This kid—this mere baby—had taken him so completely off balance that he couldn't think of a word to say. She, however, seemed entirely at ease. One bare arm lay on the table, the small hand relaxed, the brown fingers tapering off to pointed, crimson nails. Her head, balanced on the slim brown neck, was inclined slightly toward him, and those strange, lovely eyes never left his face. He thought, She's going to be beautiful one of these days. When she grows up. When I am a doctor.

Then he thought, She's beautiful now. It had hit him just like that. He was going to come back and marry Shelley Carew. When she grew up. When he had finished school.

He was conscious now of a discreet tap on the door, a sound bringing him back from the past to the present. Miss Williams, her nurse's cap straight and stiff on her gray hair, opened the door.

"Mrs. Barnes to see you, Doctor," she said.

Larry Beckwith's day had started.

Martha Donnell sat in Dr. Beckwith's waiting room, feeling more relief than regret that her turn would not come immediately. She found a child's picture book for her nephew, and the child sat regarding it docilely but with little enthusiasm. Poor little Clark—if he just weren't so outside of things, she thought. He didn't know how to get along with other children, acting as if they were a different race from himself. He wasn't at ease with adults either, and try as she would to make him feel she loved him and wanted him, he still didn't seem sure of her. Of course, it was hard for a child to be shifted around from pillar to post, always staying with somebody strange to him instead of with his mother, who usually was—well, not able to look after him. Most of the time, or so Martha had gathered from the things Clark said, he had stayed with distant relatives, who kept him only because they thought they'd get paid for doing it and, when the money failed to come, shifted him off to someone else. And when he was home with his mother, the way she was—well, that wouldn't help a child to feel sure of himself or of anyone around him.

After all, she reasoned, he hadn't been here long enough for him to become accustomed to her or to the town. Perhaps he thought this would be simply a repetition of his other experiences—stay awhile, wear out his welcome and then be sent somewhere else. She must be patient, she thought, and give him time. And lots of love.

It was cool and quiet here, with that curious sense of timelessness so often present in a doctor's waiting room. Each patient, engrossed in his own problem, made of himself a solitary unit, withdrawn and inviolate. Martha was glad of a chance to sit quietly with nothing to do; it was seldom that she had the chance.

She took a look at herself in the mirror on the opposite wall and was neither pleased nor displeased with what she saw. She was glad she had washed her hair. It was always nicer after a shampoo, the copper lights showing in the brown. She supposed she really should have her hair cut and try a new hairdo. Still, she couldn't quite bring herself to do this. Cutting might ruin the natural curl.

And if she cut her hair, she'd probably be tempted to buy some new clothes. This morning she had felt curiously dissatisfied when she looked in her closet, trying to decide what to wear. All her dresses seemed to look alike— tailored blues and blacks and grays, with touches of white. The sort of thing saleswomen called "neat." It would be fun to buy a red dress for a change, or one of those soft purples that were so stylish this season.

For a moment she considered the possibility, and then dismissed it firmly. No new clothes this fall. She had

Clark to look after. Not that she wasn't glad to have him
—he would help to fill the emptiness of the house, now that
Papa was gone. The sight of Papa's empty chair had
reached out to engulf her each time she came in. With
Clark around, she didn't notice so much.

The boy stirred in his seat beside her now, turning a
half-furtive, slightly fearful glance at her as he tentatively
closed the book, testing to see if she would allow him to
discard it or make him continue looking at it.

The poor child. There was no way of guessing all the
things he had endured before coming to her. Now and
then hints slipped out—mostly in gestures such as he had
just made—but not the whole picture. He had been with
her only a few weeks and she hadn't pressed for details.

The first night at supper he had upset his glass of
milk, which was nothing unusual for a child. She got up
from the table and came back with a cloth to mop up the
mess, her hand outstretched. He drew back in terror.

"I couldn't help it," he sobbed, and dodged as if she
were going to hit him.

"Of course you couldn't, honey," she said gently. "It's
all right. Don't cry." Her heart ached at his forlornness.
Don should have sent him to her sooner. But then, Don so
rarely did things the way he should.

That was the truth, much as Martha hated to admit
it. Sitting there in the detached quiet of Larry Beckwith's

waiting room, she tried to make herself face this fact; she tried also, a faint frown between her eyes, to think how much of this had been her fault. People said Martha Donnell had spoiled her brother, and maybe she had. Perhaps that was her way of trying to make up to him for having no mother. She did the best she could for him, but since she was a scant four years older than he was, her attempts to make a home for Don and her father had been awkward at best. Too, there was always the problem of money. She hadn't minded, but Don had.

"All the other fellows have cars," he had once blurted out to her.

"Larry Beckwith doesn't have a car."

"Oh, him!" Don dismissed the older boy curtly. And then, "I wish you didn't always throw him up to me. All I hear is 'Larry does this' and 'Larry doesn't do that.' You can't expect me to do all that he does. He's older than I am, and besides, it's not human to be as perfect as he is. As *you* think he is."

Perhaps that had been part of the trouble. She could remember, back across the years when she was seventeen and a senior in high school, how she had admired Larry.

If she was to have breakfast ready, the house in a semblance of order, and get to school on time, she had to be up very early. Usually as she was dressing she could hear the thud of the paper Larry threw on the porch and would think how much earlier he must have got up in order to pick up his papers and deliver them, for this was the end of the line for him. Another half block to go and he'd be home, where his mother would give him breakfast and some soft cluckings of sympathy—just enough to make him feel loved but not enough to start him feeling sorry for himself. Mrs. Beckwith was a good mother; that was what Don lacked.

Saturdays, when Martha worked at the five-and-ten, she could see Larry across the street at Langley's store, loading up deliveries or sweeping out or doing other odd jobs. You never saw Larry when he wasn't working. He made good grades, too. Not one to set the woods on fire, his teachers said, but good and solid and in the upper group.

Just as Martha had used to think of him on cold mornings out delivering his papers, so she had glowed at the good reports of his grades. Don had accused her once of being in love with him. She had denied it hotly—too hotly. Maybe she *had* been, a little. But even if it were true, it was ridiculous. Larry was two years younger than she, and besides, he never seemed to notice her—except as a good friend. He was too busy to bother with girls.

He zipped through school—pre-med in three years, working to supplement his GI allotment, then medical school, and then his internship. Larry Beckwith didn't have time for girls. She could understand that better than anyone, for she too, had been busy. The school board had let her start substitute teaching in Benson after one complete year of college and two summer sessions. She had got her degree and a permanent certificate by taking extension courses while she taught during the school year and going to school during the summer.

Somewhere in those crowded years Don had got away from her—if, indeed, she had ever exerted any influence on him. He went to California, where his life became a series of short-lived jobs. It was while he had worked briefly at an airplane factory that he met Janine and married her.

The newlyweds had come to Benson immediately afterward in Don's secondhand sports car, and the marvel was that it had held together until they arrived. Don indicated that new tires and an overhaul job would be an acceptable wedding gift, and Martha had financed both, admitting rather ruefully to herself that she did it to make sure they'd be able to go back to California.

But try as she would, she couldn't make herself love Janine—or, failing that, even like her. The girl had bleached hair showing dark at the roots, and vacant blue eyes deeply edged with mascara. She painted on a dark scarlet mouth in complete disregard of the way nature had shaped it, and her smile always looked as if it were inspired by adenoids rather than animation. Any of these physical features

Martha could have brought herself to overlook, but the girl's whining voice and her waspish treatment of Don were hard to take. Still, Martha told herself sensibly, Don had selected her, and his family would have to make the best of the situation.

The visit was short and far from pleasant. Janine accused Martha of disliking her—through the thin walls of her room Martha heard the indictment made in Janine's whining voice. They left the next day with new tires and refurbished engine.

Martha watched them go, torn between relief to have the girl out of the house and the distressful memory of seeing Don's harried, defensive attitude in the presence of his bride.

Clark (named for the famous movie actor who had once been kind enough to say hello to Janine when she had visited a movie lot where he was working) was born the first year of the marriage. Martha sent along a gift of money, but did not see the child until he was two, when she went to California to summer school. He was then staying with a relative because his mother was sick.

Before the summer was over, Martha knew the nature of Janine's "illness." She drank—not just socially but compulsively. The knowledge weighed on Martha's mind once she got back home. She might have thought about it more, but Papa had got sick that fall and spent the next three years alternating between his bed and his wheel chair. Last spring he had died.

Don said he couldn't come home to the funeral. Janine was sick—she had been sick off and on for months now. And that was the last Martha had heard from him until two weeks ago, when Don had called to say that he was sending Janine to a—well, it was a sort of hospital, and he wondered if it would be possible for Clark to come to Martha for a while.

"Why, of course, Don," she had said. "You know he may come. . . ."

"Miss Donnell?" Miss Williams' voice interrupted Martha's thoughts. "You and your nephew may come in now."

Clark went pale, and Martha took his hand. "It's all right, honey," she said. "Dr. Beckwith isn't going to hurt you."

Together they went into the doctor's office.

- 2 -

THE TELEPHONE ON BILL THORNDYKE'S DESK JANGLED IM-
peratively. He lifted the receiver and said, "Hello."

He felt the muscles around his mouth tighten as he
heard his wife's voice. "Bill," Ursula said without preliminary greeting, her voice thick, "Bill, I'm out of medicine."

"Yes," he said cautiously, unwilling to betray the nature
of the conversation to others who might be listening.
As if the whole town didn't know already! Hadn't known
for years!

"Did you hear me, Bill? I need some medicine."

"Yes, I'll see to it," he assured her, trying to act as if
this were an ordinary business matter, knowing quite well
that he failed in the attempt.

"You won't forget? The last time you did, and—"

"I won't forget," he promised, replacing the phone,
hoping the click was definite enough to convince her she

must not call back. Perhaps he should see to the matter immediately in order to forestall another call.

From where he sat he had only to raise his eyes to see the drugstore where he would go for the tablets which, years ago, Dr. Grayson had prescribed for Ursula. They were probably only a mild sedative; otherwise, with the stiffer drug laws now, he would not be able to have the prescription refilled without a doctor's orders. Even if, as Bill suspected, their healing power was largely in Ursula's mind, she still must have them. By now they had become as necessary to her as food itself—more so, for she ate scarcely anything.

He flicked his gaze away from the drugstore to Ben Langley's dry goods store. A man was just walking inside —a stranger, Bill thought, noting his air of mingled determination and uncertainty as to his place in the town.

It was a look, Bill Thorndyke thought, with which he himself was not unfamiliar. It did not necessarily come from being new in town. Bill had been born here, and yet, aside from business contacts he had no real place in the life of Benson. Of course, with Ursula the way she was . . .

He felt a stirring of contempt for himself that he should blame his situation on his wife, but try as he might, there was no way of separating her from it. His mind went racing back across the years to the morning when he had first met her, more than twenty years ago.

Young Bill Thorndyke was home from Austin for his summer vacation, feeling older and wiser than he was ever to feel again. He was just past twenty, his sophomore year behind him. He had gone into the bank—W. A.'s bank, the townspeople called it. His father, W. A. Thorndyke, was president, and although everyone knew it was largely Jim Carew's money that kept it going, they were well aware of the fact that W. A. had money, too—and furthermore, a shrewdness and cool inflexibility of will and judgment. People didn't mind his brusque ways. They thought this only proved he was a good watchdog for their money. Under no circumstances would they have wanted him to be a back-slapping fraternizer. If a man got a loan from W. A., it meant he had something on the ball.

His father had been sitting at his desk—this very desk, as a matter of fact—and with him was Jim Carew. Bill knew better than to interrupt a conference, especially one with Mr. Carew. He said hello to the employees, most of whom he had known since childhood, and then decided he'd go to the café across the street for a cup of coffee. There he first saw Ursula.

Part of his defense, now and always, was that he had never seen a more beautiful girl. Add up all the clichés about beauty—golden hair, big blue eyes behind smoky lashes, rosy skin, tantalizing figure—and there she was. There was also about her a certain breathless excitement, as if she wanted to tell someone what a wonderful place the café was, and the town, and the world. He gulped a couple of times, not believing his own eyes. And then she was at his side.

"May I help you?" she asked in a low, curiously shy voice.

"Uh," he stammered, "I want—I mean, uh, bring me some coffee." Then he added awkwardly, like a boy caught in a breach of manners, "Please."

"Yes, sir," she said.

Her voice, although not a cultured one, had a charming upward lilt. She was back with his coffee while he was still trying vainly to think of some way to engage her in conversation. Before any idea came to him, she had gone back to stand behind the counter.

It came to him that she was not only the most beautiful girl he had ever seen, but that she was apparently unaware of her looks. Any other girl, possessing even half her beauty, would have preened and giggled. Not this one.

There were any number of ways he might have found out about her, but he chose the most convenient one. Finished with his coffee, he went across the street to the library and there, without any pretense of beating about the bush said, "Who's the new girl at Martin's, Miss Stacie?"

"Now you keep away from her, Bill Thorndyke," Stacie Sheperd ordered, taking off her glasses and pulling vigorously at the chain so that it disappeared with a zip into the button on her blouse front. "Away. Hear me?"

"You mean, you don't know her?" he asked guilelessly.

Miss Stacie, put on her mettle by the very suggestion, gave details.

The girl was Ursula Malone, and she had come to town just after Christmas to live with the Martins. She was Mrs. Martin's niece—or rather, half-niece, for she was Mrs. Martin's half-brother's daughter. And that half-brother was a shiftless lout and never could make a living for his family, and so the Martins took Ursula in, and wasn't it decent of them? And Ursula was a good girl and not spoiled at all, and after she got off work she often came by the library and checked out books.

"Of course, they aren't what you'd call real literature," Miss Stacie admitted reluctantly. "Kathleen Norris and Zane Grey and Grace S. Richmond. But I did get her to read *Little Women*, and last week she checked out *Treasure Island*. I have hopes for her. And she never misses church. The Martins let her have Sunday off."

"Well, thanks, Miss Stacie," Bill said, standing up.

"Remember what I said—no fooling around," she called after him as he walked away.

"Is it all right if I go over and read *Little Women* with her?" he asked.

Miss Stacie laughed delightedly.

28

The Man Who Told the Truth

Back at the bank, he couldn't keep his mind on what he was doing. Whereas once he might have been proud to have his father and Jim Carew stand up and shake hands with him, now all he could think of was how to meet that extraordinary girl across the street. Ursula Malone, half-niece of Mrs. Martin, daughter of a shiftless father— and so beautiful that just thinking about her made his head swim.

Meeting her, while requiring a bit of planning, was not really very difficult. Benson was small enough so that few people could give themselves any airs. From Jim Carew down, everyone was vocally proud of the fact that everyone was just as good as everyone else. Only after one got to know the place did he see the gaps that existed— the taboos, the cliques, the class consciousness—all made the more cruel because in a town as small as this they were impossible to miss, even by the very people who most stubbornly denied their existence.

As a matter of fact, Bill Thorndyke had met Ursula in the most approved fashion—at church, in a Sunday School class of young people taught by Bess Dawson. During the lesson Bill watched Ursula, sitting a little to the left and in front of him. He had entertained some sort of half-fear that she might not look as good in street clothes as she did in a uniform. In this, he was only partly right. Her blue dress was a little on the fussy side, but acceptable.

Her white hat had a little too much of everything, but you didn't notice that when you saw the face beneath it.

Mrs. Dawson herself performed the introduction. "Ursula," she said, "this is Bill Thorndyke, home from college. His father's in the bank, you know."

It was almost as if Bess Dawson were saying, Watch it, my girl. I'm giving you all the details, so you just remember your place.

"Hello," Ursula said, lifting her lovely blue eyes to look unself-consciously into his face. "I've already met Mr. Thorndyke."

So she remembered him.

"Oh, sure," he said.

When she started out the door he fell in step with her, feeling Bess Dawson's speculative eyes on him as he did so.

That was the start—bright and lovely, a thing so filled with tremulous beauty and excitement that it shut out the whole world. Now, twenty-odd years later, it had narrowed down to a relationship that asked only that he bring home the pills to lessen her pain.

He shrugged his shoulders and began to rearrange the papers on his desk. This pile must be turned over to Shelley Carew, already at her desk in the small office that had been assigned to her in the bank when she decided that she would take over her father's affairs after his death.

"I know very little about business of any sort," she had

said gravely when she came in for her first conference with Bill. "Least of all about my father's affairs. But I want to try to learn."

Bill Thorndyke had considered this a very commendable decision on her part and had told her so. Still, he had thought her interest would die down as soon as she realized the complicated and far-flung nature of her father's affairs, but it had not. Knowing it would be a long pull, she had decided to establish her mother—more vague and helpless than ever, now that her husband was gone—in an apartment in Dallas with a good nurse and a middle-aged cousin to look after things. Shelley herself would divide her time between Dallas and Benson, since there was much business to be seen to in both places.

Looking back on the matter now, Bill wondered that he had been surprised at her decision to take over herself— or that, having once decided, she should have gone about the complicated work with such single-minded purpose and so intelligent a grasp of business details. She was her father's daughter. Almost invariably her decisions paralleled closely the approach her father had usually taken. Nowhere was this more apparent than in her decision about the town philanthropies that Jim Carew had long taken care of personally. In almost the first conference Bill had with Shelley he mentioned these.

"As you know," he said, "your father financed a great

many projects in town. We have been administering these according to his instructions. Would you like to look them over? Perhaps discontinue a few?"

After all, their combined cost was rather large. A young girl might have other ideas about spending the money, Bill thought.

Shelley made a quick, denying gesture. "No," she said. "Those were dear to him. We'll let them go, at least for the present."

"I must tell you that they are both extensive and expensive," he warned her.

"All the more reason I should turn my attention to other things first. Unless the rest of the business goes well, we might have to drop some of them, and I know my father wouldn't have wanted that."

"That's right," Bill admitted.

"Very well, go ahead supporting his charities just as you have all along. When I get a grasp of the business itself, then I'll turn to them."

That's the way matters stood now. The bank continued to pay out money to the many good causes Jim Carew had underwritten, and Shelley waded through the mazes of figures and facts having to do with ranch and oil holdings and the other properties making up the bulk of the estate.

Bill could see Shelley now, her head bent over the

papers on her desk. He could leave without saying good morning to her, but it seemed a bleak way to begin the day. Since he had to go across to the drugstore anyway, and since it would be just as easy to go out by the door nearest the room she used for an office, he'd speak to her on his way out.

He rose from his chair and made his way across the polished floor to the room where she worked. She looked up and smiled as he came in—the quick glinting smile that made crinkled lines at the corners of her eyes and softened the contours of her mouth.

"Well," she said gaily, "you look grave this morning. Don't tell me Dad promised to underwrite the United Nations?"

In spite of himself and forgetting for a moment the errand that lay before him, he laughed.

"I may run across that item later," he told her. "No, I just dropped by to say good morning and ask if there is anything I can do for you."

"Well, not just now. But thanks, anyway."

He stood there uncertainly a moment, trying to think of some excuse to prolong his stay, but failing to hit upon one, he turned and left her.

That evening Miss Stacie Sheperd—stopping by Bess Dawson's on her way home after the library had closed—

had much news to report. The stranger was named Paul Mitchell. He had indeed gone to Daisy Higdon's and Daisy had agreed to provide him with room and board. He had paid a week in advance. Some of these days—in Miss Stacie's opinion—Daisy would be murdered in her bed, taking in strangers like that with no recommendation from anyone she knew. Daisy did say, however, that Mr. Mitchell was clean and neat and as well-mannered as she could ask for—even if he didn't offer much information about himself. He said he liked the looks of the town and decided he'd stay on awhile, and asked if she knew of any work he could get. Daisy asked him what his line was, and he said a lot of things. And when she asked, "Like what?" he told her his last job had been clerking in a store.

So of course Daisy told him Ben Langley was looking for someone, since Max Butler was leaving for college in a week or two. And the stranger—Paul Mitchell—had gone over and talked to Ben, and what did Ben do, but give him a job. Just like that. And wasn't Ben Langley taking a chance? Miss Stacie asked now. The stranger could steal him blind.

Mrs. Dawson said mildly that she guessed Ben Langley knew what he was about, and anyway, he himself was always there first thing in the morning and was the last to leave at night and so he could keep an eye on the cash register. Maybe things would work out now so Ben and Hallie could go to Florida this winter. And Miss Stacie said yes, maybe things would work out, and went on to talk of other matters.

She said Martha Donnell had gone to see Larry Beckwith that morning. It was too bad for Martha to have her nephew on her hands just at a time when she might have got out and had a little fun for herself.

And then she said she had seen Bill Thorndyke go into the drugstore, and she guessed Ursula was having one of her spells again. And they said, "Poor Bill," in unison.

"I don't know that I can find it in my heart to blame her, though," Bess Dawson said. "The way my arthritis has been acting up today, I'd have taken almost anything I could have laid my hands on. I called Larry and he just gave me that old aspirin routine."

"You poor thing," Miss Stacie said. "Would it help if I gave you an alcohol rub before I left?"

"Oh, shucks no, you're too tired."

"I'm no such thing."

She helped her friend disrobe and then, once the invalid was in bed, began to rub her back.

Under her fingers she could feel the slight recoil of her friend's muscles, knew the rubbing was causing momentary pain, even if the final result would be good. So she started a running comment on the town's news.

"Shelley Carew got back last night," she said.

"Oh, she did, did she?"

"Yes—I saw her standing at the door of the bank, as if she hated the thought of going in. Then all of a sudden she just raised her chin real high and in she sailed."

"Sounds like her father," Bess Dawson said. "Wonder if she and Larry ever see each other?"

"Don't ask me," Miss Stacie said. "Wonder whatever happened between them anyway. Everybody thought they were going to be married, and then—bang! It blew up right in our faces."

"Could have been most anything," Bess Dawson said. "They're both so proud and headstrong, any quarrel was bound to be a dilly."

"For heaven's sake, Stacie," Bess interrupted herself, "leave me some hide. I need it to hold my old bones together."

Miss Stacie laughed, stopped her rubbing, and pulled the covers gently over her friend.

"Good night," she said softly. "I'll see you tomorrow . . ."

- 3 -

MISS STACIE ALWAYS SAID OCTOBER WAS THE NICEST MONTH of all in Texas; there were few who would give her an argument. The sky, scoured clear of summer's dust by early fall rains, seemed too blue to be real. The wind was content to settle down to a mild zephyr. Each morning the sun rose out of a crimson sky, shone benignly all day and then sank in a multicolored sunset in the evening. Everyone greeted everyone else with, "Did you *ever* see such weather!"

Only Ben Langley, on his way to his store, took no part in the general rejoicing. Weather like this was bad for business, lulling people into the false notion that summer would last forever and that therefore they needn't stock up on winter clothes. It was ironic that now, just when he had a good salesman at last, he had almost no customers.

It had taken Ben Langley only a few days to see that he had first-class help in Paul Mitchell. It was apparent, really, from the first morning, when Ben had found his new clerk at the store early, waiting for him to unlock.

"You're early," Ben said mildly, reserving judgment.

"I was out taking a look at the town," Mitchell explained. "It's a nice place. Reminds me of a town I used to know."

"Where?" Ben asked politely, leading the way into the dimly lighted store. This was a moment he always enjoyed—entering the store to sniff its mingled odors of dry goods, shoe leather and cosmetics. His store was his world. He wasn't sure he'd like the idea of sharing the experience with the new clerk, just in case Mitchell made up his mind to be waiting at the door every morning.

"Oh, I've lived in a lot of places," Mitchell said.

Ben Langley faced the man quickly. Did he have a fugitive on his payroll, a potential thief or worse? Mitchell bore the scrutiny with complete indifference, if not unawareness. The man might be evasive, Ben decided, but not criminal or furtive. A good honest face. Strong features. There was a certain standoffishness about him, granted, but then people sometimes assumed a kind of aloofness as protective coloring when things got a bit thick for them—Bill Thorndyke, for instance, when Ursula was having one of her bad times. Still, Ben thought, you had to check a bit on a new employee, especially one who came with no references.

"You said you'd had experience clerking in a store,"

he said, rather more brusquely than he intended.

Mitchell, apparently choosing to believe Ben's sharpness had nothing to do with him, answered mildly. "Yes. I was working in a store before I came here," he said.

He paused, a hesitation Ben Langley felt was not for purposes of concealment. Paul Mitchell ran his hand across his forehead, and then suddenly his face brightened. "In a small town in Kansas," he said. "Heathville. I was trying to remember the owner's name. It was an unusual one—Czyconia, it was. You can write to him if you wish."

"Oh, that's all right," Ben said. So long as Mitchell did his work satisfactorily, he thought . . . But all the same, he was going to keep a close watch on things.

Ben reached for the light switch and there it was— his store. Even the dust covers did not detract from the wonder of it—adding, rather, a sense of mystery and charm to the place.

"Have you ever thought of installing a new lighting system?" Mitchell asked suddenly. "The place seems a little dark. People probably can't see the merchandise as well as they might."

Ben Langley felt a twinge of annoyance. This stranger had hit upon something that he himself had felt vaguely but had never been quite able, or willing, to put into words. His first impulse was to tell Paul Mitchell to mind his own business. To his surprise, he retorted mildly, "Yes, I'd sort of thought of that myself. . . . You can work over here in the men's department," Ben went on. "Good thing you came early. You can get acquainted with the stock."

Maybe some people would call him a fool for trusting this stranger, he had thought then, but he'd had a strong hunch that the man would be a good salesman. That's what he wanted, wasn't it?

Now, in October, Ben Langley was all the more sure he had hired a good man. He had long since grown accustomed to finding Paul Mitchell waiting for him at the door in the mornings. It had got to be a fairly pleasant routine, opening the door and standing back to let Mitchell enter first. The man seemed to sense instinctively that it was never his place to turn on the lights—even though by now Ben had installed new ones, as his clerk had suggested.

"Looks like we're going to have another summer day," Ben said glumly now.

"Yes," Mitchell agreed. "Now, last year . . ."

Ben scarcely noticed that Mitchell's words came to a dead stop. He had grown accustomed to this mannerism in his clerk and accepted it. Most people talked too much about themselves anyway, he thought.

Martha Donnell stuffed the ungraded papers into her briefcase. There had been a time when she stayed at her desk until she finished, but this year was different. She needed to be home as soon as she could, for Clark got out at two and she hated leaving him alone. True, Mrs. Beckwith would run across the street and look in on him, but all the same . . .

She took her purse and a light sweater from the locker, said good night to the janitor and then walked out into the blue-gold afternoon. Children played in vacant lots, calling to each other—batting balls and shooting marbles just as if it were spring. She wished that Clark were among them, but as yet he couldn't seem to make himself a part of a group. She consoled herself by thinking of how much better he was than when he had come to her.

When she had taken him to Larry Beckwith for that first examination she had half-expected to be told something was physically wrong with the child. A weak heart, maybe, or incipient t.b., or something. She had indicated as much when she telephoned for the appointment, wanting Larry to know that Clark needed more than just the routine preschool shots.

Larry, accordingly, had given the child a thorough going over. Clark accepted it as he accepted everything—a procedure he had to submit to whether he liked it or not. If only the child weren't so apathetic, Martha thought, so frightened of everyone.

Finished with the examination, Larry said, "Okay, fel-

low, you're in fine shape. Go out into that room there—
the one where Miss Williams is—and tell her she's to give
you those shots. Just like they give soldiers in the Army."

He punched the boy lightly in the ribs. Clark dodged
as if he were in mortal danger, turning a sickly white.

"Oh, it won't hurt," Larry assured him, looking at the
child through slightly narrowed eyes. "And you tell her I
said you are to have the lollipop before, not after, she
shoots you."

Clark went obediently to the door where Miss Williams
waited, and Larry indicated by a slight gesture that Martha
was to stay.

"Kid's had a pretty rough time, I'd say," he said.

"Oh, yes . . ." Martha was grateful that Larry had
caught on without her having to tell the whole disgraceful
story. "Yes, he has."

"You're a great gal, Martha," he told her, his kind,
strong face filled with admiration. He reached across the
desk to put his hand over hers, and she felt her heart begin
to race so wildly she thought he'd hear it.

"Oh, shut up," she said thickly.

What a stupid thing for her to say, she thought, when
all the time she wanted nothing more than to have him go
on praising her. She snatched her hand away to dab
quickly at her eyes with a handkerchief.

"You'll snap him out of it," Larry went on casually.

"I'll help all I can. Don't expect miracles, though. Just be glad that organically he's perfectly all right."

"Is there anything I should do? Specifically, that is?"

"Well, see that he gets the right food and plenty of rest. I suspect he's had neither for a long time, if ever. I don't need to tell you to be patient with him. He needs plenty of T.L.C."

"Tender loving care," she said a little shakily. "You sound like my child-psychology books."

"I read them myself," he told her. "Of course you know he may not like school at first. He's had no real reason as yet to feel people are going to love him."

"He's been pretty well pushed around from one place to another," Martha admitted.

"Yes. It shows. Well, as I said, we'll all help you wherever we can."

He stood then, indicating the interview was over, and she stood too and went toward the room where Nurse Williams was giving Clark his shots.

"Take care of yourself, Martha," Larry told her gently. "You're not indestructible, you know."

"Oh, I'm fine," she said.

And so she was, suddenly. Just fine.

She did the best she could with Clark. At first she hadn't particularly liked having to get up so early on

Sunday—the only day she could really sleep late—in order
to take him to Sunday School. But she knew it was a good
idea, so she got up before eight, cooked a good breakfast
for the two of them and then took him to Sunday School.
Once or twice she had considered sending him alone—the
church was only three blocks away, and many of the other
children went by themselves—but almost immediately she
discarded the idea. After the first few Sundays Clark
seemed to like going. And once she was up and about, she
didn't mind either. She did decide, however, that it might
be a good idea to have their Sunday dinner at Daisy Higdon's. It would be a chance for Clark to be with people,
as well as a way of giving herself a rest.

The first time they went something unusual had happened. When they walked into the dining room Paul
Mitchell was already there, standing at the window looking
out on the street. When he turned and saw them at the
door, a strange expression came over his face. Martha had
never quite identified it. Fear? Disbelief? A drawing recognition—as if perhaps he might remember having known
Clark before he came here? Whatever it was, Martha
had the feeling that he was ready to flee the room, and
might have done so if she and Clark had not been standing in one doorway and Daisy in the other. The expression lasted only a moment, then he seemed himself once
more.

"So this is your nephew," he said easily, as if his strange behavior had been a product of Martha's imagination. "I've been hearing about him."

"Clark, this is Mr. Mitchell," Martha said, hoping the child would not be timid and frightened.

"Hi," Clark said, regarding Paul Mitchell gravely. "Aunt Martha said we might have chicken."

Martha gave a slight start. It was the first time she had heard Clark take the initiative in a conversation.

"And so we are," Paul assured him. "I peeked into the kitchen. We'll see that you get the wishbone."

After that, the two of them—Paul Mitchell and Clark —became good friends. Occasionally the man would come across to the porch where Martha and Clark sat on warm September evenings and talk with the child as if he were a fellow adult. This pleased Clark, already accustomed to life with his elders. He saved his treasures—a striped lizard, a chipped marble, an odd rock—to show his friend. At first, Martha watched them closely, remembering in spite of herself Paul Mitchell's strange behavior that first day. But gradually she forgot this and accepted him for what he seemed to be—a man genuinely interested in Clark.

As a matter of fact, she found herself looking forward to his visits. It was pleasant to sit in the porch swing and have him there on the step below her, talking to Clark in his deep voice, sometimes turning to speak idly to her about nothing in particular.

She knew there was gossip about them in the town. Well, let them talk, Martha thought. For years people had been trying to marry her off—and, as they said, they could have done it a dozen times if only she had cooperated a little. What was wrong with her, anyway? people asked her. Didn't she want to marry and have a home of her own? Did she really prefer to teach school, spending her time looking after other women's children?

Approaching her house she quickened her step and saw Clark hurrying to meet her.

"Some wild ducks flew over," he said breathlessly when he reached her. "They were going south. Mrs. Beckwith made me some hot chocolate."

"What fun," she said.

"Did you bring me anything?"

"A sling shot," she said. "I took it away from a big boy. I told him I was going to bring it to you, and he said that was all right."

"What's a sling shot?" he asked.

Of course he wouldn't know, she thought. That was one of the sad things—he had so little of childhood's natural heritage.

"I'll show you," she said. "We'll make you a target."

"If it's something to shoot with, I want Mr. Mitchell to show me," Clark told her. "Dr. Larry says he's one of the best shots in town."

The Man Who Told the Truth

Larry Beckwith stretched out full length, reveling in the comfort of staying in bed late. Well, seven thirty seemed late to him. The last few Sundays he had been up before dawn to take Paul Mitchell quail hunting, an enterprise instigated by his mother.

"Paul Mitchell's been dropping by Martha's house rather often," Mrs. Beckwith had begun obliquely.

"Mom," he accused her solemnly, "you're getting as bad as Miss Stacie."

"Since Martha doesn't have any men in her family," Mrs. Beckwith went on unperturbed, "I thought maybe somebody ought to—well, sort of check."

"To see if he means right by Martha?" Larry asked.

"No. To see if he—well, just means right, *period*. After all, we don't know a living thing about him," she pointed out sensibly. "And they say Martha does seem interested."

Larry grinned at her. "Oh, all right, Mom," he said. "I'll ask him to go quail hunting with me tomorrow. If I get shot in the back, you've only yourself to blame."

Actually, he admitted to himself, his mother was right. Martha was a wonderful girl—none better—but she was hopelessly naïve and trusting. Perhaps he *should* have a look at this man who was hanging around. After all, nobody knew a cotton-picking thing about Paul Mitchell's life before he came to Benson. Everybody who had tried to find out had had the same experience—they'd run up against a blank wall. Oh, the guy was polite enough, Larry reflected, and well-mannered, but a mystery man all the same. As much for Clark's sake as for Martha's, he ought to find out a little bit more about this newcomer.

It was in this spirit that he began their association. He continued it because he really liked the man—which was strange, for he had got no closer to Paul Mitchell than any of the others had. Mitchell was reticent, occasionally almost to the point of rudeness. For instance, on their first quail hunt, Larry had noticed a long, thin scar back of Mitchell's right ear. As a doctor, he immediately felt a professional interest in it and was moved to say, "Pretty bad scar there back of your ear. Happen recently?"

Paul Mitchell ran a finger tentatively across the red line. More than anything else, he registered surprise at finding it there—as if, Larry thought, it had slipped up on him in the night. At first it seemed that he did not intend to answer, but finally he said, "Oh, not too long ago," and changed the subject.

There were other surprises before the day was over. Larry, wanting to cut across a pasture, said to Mitchell, "Say—why don't you just bring the car around to the road and meet me there."

Mitchell looked almost panicky. "I don't drive."

So Larry himself drove the car, Paul Mitchell sitting beside him and neither saying a word.

Before the day was over, however, Larry was accepting

48

Mitchell on his own terms. He was reserved, certainly, but he was not really evasive. Larry, who spent most of his time listening to people turning their souls wrongside out for him to have a look, found it refreshing to encounter a little healthy reserve.

Gradually he came to the conclusion that Paul Mitchell for all his unwillingness to talk about himself, was just about as normal as most people and more so than some he could name! In his judgment, it was quite all right for Mitchell to be around Clark and Martha. She could even do worse than to marry him, as Miss Stacie was archly hinting she might do. For a moment Larry even considered promoting the idea, but on second thought he decided to keep out of it. Martha was gallant and courageous, facing life as it came to her, doing the best she could. If she had little choice in the things she must do, did anyone have a great choice?

Lying there in bed that morning, Larry considered the matter gravely. He seldom had time to give thought to his own problems; he had a feeling of justifiable selfishness as he did so now. Yesterday afternoon as he stood for a moment at the door of his office he had seen Shelley Carew leave the bank and walk across the street toward her car. His heart had followed her every step; he wondered if she could fail to sense it. And ever since, he had been thinking about her.

Just the sight of her had the power to move him like that. In the first months following the breakup of their engagement, he had tried halfheartedly to find some other girl. Lord knows there'd been no lack of opportunity, he thought wryly, with all his friends trying to make a match and mothers fairly throwing their daughters at his head. Even his own mother had begun praising this or that girl, saying what a good doctor's wife she'd make. The catch was that he couldn't help comparing them all to Shelley, and invariably they couldn't measure up.

He loved her that much, yet he was the one who, over a year ago, had broken the engagement. If he had it to do over, would he act differently? He doubted it. Now, as then, he felt he had no choice—even though they had been planning to marry for more than five years.

Late in the summer in the year he was to enter medical school he had come home for a brief vacation. Shelley, too, was home, getting ready to return to her college in Vermont. Knowing she was home, Larry called to ask if he might come over, and she said, "Of course, silly—why do you even ask?"

He hadn't seen her for nearly a year and should have been able to think of something sensible to say when she opened the door to him, but all he managed was, "Well, you've certainly grown up!" Whereupon she laughed—probably remembering, as he did, what she had once said about his marrying her when she grew up. Well, there was no denying she was grown up now, and though she was not beautiful she was an unusually attractive girl.

"I hoped you'd notice," she said, looking at him directly. "Come on—say hello to Mom and Dad."

She led the way into the living room. Jim Carew greeted him with a bluff and hearty "Hello, Larry," and a handshake. Mrs. Carew, vague and frail, seemed even less capable than she had used to be of understanding her husband, her daughter or even herself. She said, "Hello, Larry," and patted his arm. "It's good to see you. But haven't you—well—grown?"

"He got that out of the way ten years ago, Mom," Shelley told her gently.

"Oh, is that right? Well, I hadn't noticed how tall you were until today. You're a good-looking boy, Larry. You look like your father did."

Across her head Shelley shot Larry a brief sardonic grin, doubtless remembering the time she fought the girl for saying he was ugly.

Mrs. Carew's forgetfulness seemed to cause her concern. Her husband took her hand and said, "All right, Mama, let's go watch TV. Your program is coming up in a few minutes."

Even a less sensitive young man than Larry Beckwith would have known they had orders beforehand to clear out once he got there, a command they followed with pleasure. He felt his ears turn red—not so much at the thought and what it implied as at the fact that with any other boy Shelley would have said, "So long, folks, we're gone . . ." and taken off in her date's car.

Larry Beckwith did not have a car. As a matter of fact, he had not even had the price of a bus ticket home. One of his friends had happened to be driving up toward Benson and had given him a ride. At the moment he had in his pocket only enough money for his share of the food, gas and oil for the trip back.

Unless you tried it, Larry thought, you couldn't know how much money it took to go to school—any kind of school, but medical school was about the most expensive of all. He had his GI Bill money, of course, and he worked. He managed to get by. At the end of every month he came out with a couple of dollars to spare, but that was about it. Once or twice he had thought he'd have to give up, when something like having to buy a new pair of shoes wrecked his budget. But he had stuck it out.

He didn't see how the married students managed. Well, yes, he did. He had only to look at the faces of the young wives—living in barracks, counting every dime six times before they turned it loose, looking tired and worn and a little soured on life—to see that this wasn't right for a woman. At the other extreme, of course, were the more prosperous ones; either the wife had a full-time job or the couple's parents subsidized them. He couldn't decide which approach he liked least.

"You're not much of a talker tonight," Shelley broke in, a mocking note in her voice. "Miss Stacie would say the cat had your tongue."

She got up and moved toward him, and on the soft carpet of the Carew's living room her steps made no sound at all. She wore, he noticed, a dress that looked simple enough, but even he could tell it was expensive. It was sleeveless with a low neck, orange-red in color. He never ceased to marvel that a girl as small-boned as she, as long-legged, should have such beautifully rounded arms, such a delicate, firm neck. He watched her, fascinated, as she came toward him, her purpose as clear and definite as it used to be when she announced she was going to follow him around his paper route.

It was no surprise at all to find that without any preliminary words she was in his arms.

For one sense-stunned second he stood there, making no move to kiss her or hold her closer. Then, as if all the inhibitions of years had fallen away, he tightened his arms around her and bent his lips to hers. What he had lacked in original purpose he gained now in force and momentum. He didn't have any notion at all of how long they stood so, nor did he care. Oddly enough, although it had been Shelley who had initiated the embrace, it was she who first broke away.

"Well," she said in a voice that shook a little, although it had a trace of the old cool mockery, "well . . . you're pretty good once you get started."

He tried to pull her back into his arms.

She stepped aside lightly but did reach out to take his hand. "All right," she said, "now let's go talk to Dad."

He jerked his hand away and whirled to face her.

"Don't look so surprised, stupid," she said gaily. "Don't you know I've been waiting since I was ten for you to kiss me? Now let's go tell Mom and Dad we're going to be married."

"Shelley—look . . ." he began in protest.

An expression he had never seen before crossed her face. It was surprise and impatience, but it was more than that. A certain childlike hurt was there, and a vulnerability he had never before sensed in her. Instinctively he reached out to draw her back into his arms. For a long time they stood quietly, and this time it was tenderness that marked their embrace. Finally he released her, and when he did he knew that he, not she, was master of the situation.

"Shelley," he said softly, "I love you. Always have, I guess."

"I know," she said, almost in a whisper.

"But, Shelley, I can't marry you now."

She jerked away from him, the old Shelley once more—arrogant, imperious, furious at being thwarted. "I don't see why! You just said you loved me!"

"So I did. And I do. But I'm not going to marry until I'm through medical school. That's settled."

"But Dad can—"

"Hush," he said harshly.

Let Old Man Carew put him through school? Not if he knew what he was doing, he wouldn't! A kept man, that's what he'd be—sponging off his wife's father.

"But he wants to," Shelley said earnestly. "I shouldn't tell you this—you're smug enough already—but he says any girl would be lucky to get you."

"And if you wanted me, he'd get me for you." Larry's voice sounded harsh, even in his own ears.

Shelley's oblique glance only deepened his conviction that Jim Carew had used almost those exact words.

"I won't do it," he told her. And then, again, even more loudly, "I won't, Shelley!"

Later he came to realize that his vehemence was entirely out of proportion to the importance of his declaration. He could have been firm without blowing his top. At the time he did not fully understand—perhaps he still did not—the complex factors underlying his attitude. Probably they went far back into his childhood—to his father, who had died when Larry was five.

Even now when people in Benson referred to Beck Beckwith, more often than not they would smile affectionately and say, "Beck was quite a fellow."

That's the way they still remembered him—gay, good-looking, brave. A man who could ride faster, shoot straighter, jump higher, throw a ball farther than anyone else in the county. In the six years after he came to Benson with his bride, he became Jim Carew's foreman, fathered a son and performed enough spectacular feats to make a legend of himself after his death. Even his death became a legend—a sort of saga of courage and daring.

Jim Carew and Beck had gone out to a far pasture to look after some cattle. A killer blizzard, swift and unheralded, roared down out of the Rockies, catching them miles from anywhere. The little pickup truck stalled in the snow. Of course, it was Beck who said he'd go for help, leaving Jim Carew—the older man—in the pickup.

After hours of wandering, going through what must have been acute torture from the cold, Beck reached a house and sent back the necessary aid to Carew, who was still safe in the cab of the pickup.

Beck Beckwith had saved his boss's life, but in so doing had caught pneumonia and died.

Young Larry Beckwith, watching his mother's grief, nursed in his heart the conviction that Mr. Carew was

responsible for his father's death. The older man had sat
in the truck, hadn't he, safe and warm, while Beck gave
his life to get help? When the town went into public
mourning for its favorite son, it never occurred to Larry
to doubt that everyone shared his resentment toward Jim
Carew.

Later, when he was older, he got the thing straight in
his mind and ceased to hold his childish grudge. Or perhaps he only thought he had, for he never was able to
acccpt without inner protest the things Jim Carew did for
the Beckwiths. A kindly man under any circumstances,
Carew would certainly have felt a deep sense of responsibility for a family who, through him, had lost a bread-
winner. The fact that he had not wanted Beck to make
the trip did not lessen his concern, which took various
forms. A deed to the house the Beckwiths lived in—Beck,
never one to be careful in business matters, had fallen far
behind in his payments. This Mrs. Beckwith accepted
graciously, doubtless seeing the necessity of allowing Mr.
Carew some generous gesture to ease his feeling of responsibility. She did, however, refuse a cash settlement, doing
so with such gentle firmness as to leave Jim Carew power-
less to insist.

"But you have a child to look after," he reminded her.

"I have a home to bring him up in," she said. "I'll
manage."

She spoke quietly, but in her voice and words Jim Carew recognized a stubbornness equal to his own and so did not press the matter. But if Mrs. Beckwith would accept no money, he never ceased to find other ways to help. Meat, vegetables, fruit, game and other products from the Carew ranch found their way to the Beckwith table. From the ranch, too, came the annual Christmas tree, which in time became to Larry a symbol of Mr. Carew's generosity. It was always too tall, too big in every way for the Beckwith living room, and only after a struggle with axe and saw were he had his mother able to cut it down to a manageable size.

"Oh, dear," his mother sighed one year, "if he'd just let us buy our own, I'd have a small one on the table."

She had cut her finger trying to lop off a couple of feet at the base of the tree while Larry sat on it in order to hold it firm.

Larry asked—very sensibly, he thought—why she didn't tell Mr. Carew how she felt. And when she said she didn't have the heart, Larry said *he* would; then Ida Beckwith said if he—Larry—breathed a word to Mr. Carew, she'd thrash him, even if it was Christmas.

And that was the way they left the matter. In time Larry got big enough to take care of the tree himself, but he never quite overcame the desire to tell Mr. Carew that the Beckwiths wished he'd stop doing so much for them.

After so long a time, he was fed up with the constant need to be grateful.

Dead, Beck Beckwith became a legend to the people of Benson; living, Ida Beckwith remained what they had always said she was—a wonderful woman. She could make the best cakes in town and did so, netting a tidy sum from women who were either unable or unwilling to make their own. She was an accomplished seamstress and was always in demand to make alterations. Children clung to her, and you had to speak a long time ahead if you wanted her to baby-sit. And as far as most of Benson was concerned, when they were sick they'd rather have Ida take care of them than any registered nurse.

For several months when Larry was in his early teens he grew accustomed to coming home to find his mother gone, his meal on the table or in the oven, with a note saying that she was at the Carews' and would be home as soon as she could.

Usually she was home by bedtime, but once or twice she spent the night, explaining that Mr. Carew was out of town on business and Mrs. Carew was not resting well.

He didn't tell her she looked as if she needed rest herself, his boy's pride reminding him that if he was old enough to notice that, he should be able to do something about it. And so he would roam restlessly about the house, strangely lonely and empty without Mom, and then finally

59

go off to bed with a feeling of resentment toward Old Man Carew, who had only to say the word in order to have Mom hop. The Beckwiths, he thought, had done quite enough for the Carews already.

He saw now it was mainly adolescent rebellion that had made him lash out against life in general and Mr. Carew in particular. And yet he realized, too, that those old memories were probably at the bottom of his quick, emphatic rejection of Shelley's suggestion that her father put him through medical school.

Shelley herself saved the situation from complete chaos by her own attitude.

" 'So he huffed and he puffed and he blew the house in,' " she quoted with gentle mockery. Then almost immediately she was contrite. "Larry," she said, "don't let's fuss. Just after—well, after things have been so wonderful."

He took her in his arms once more and after a while they were able to discuss the matter calmly. He would get through medical school on his own. Shelley would go back to college somewhere—not Vermont; it was too far away. California, maybe.

So they left the matter there. He couldn't give her his fraternity pin to wear because he didn't belong to a fraternity—that was a luxury he had had to forgo. But all the same, they knew they were engaged to be engaged. . . .

All these memories crowded in on Larry Beckwith now, lying in bed this Sunday morning in October. He had gone back over his life, coming full circle to the present. And all he got out of it was a conviction that dredging up the past got you nowhere—psychiatrists to the contrary. The one conclusion he had reached was that somewhere along the line he had jolly well made a hash of things.

URSULA THORNDYKE WAS HAVING WHAT WAS, FOR HER, A VERY good breakfast indeed: orange juice, a poached egg, toast and coffee. She couldn't remember when she had bothered to cook an egg for herself or when food had tasted so good. Perhaps the fact that she had slept better than usual had something to do with her appetite. Only one pill, too. Sometimes she had to get up in the night and take a second one.

She supposed it came of having spent a pleasant evening last night. The new man in town, Paul Mitchell, had dropped by, unexpected and uninvited. It was still early—just eight o'clock—but even so, she had been considering going to bed. She and Bill were in the den, but not talking. They never seemed to have much to say to each other these days. He was reading the paper, so she didn't turn on the television; that always disturbed him, although he didn't come right out and tell her so. Then a knock come at the door and she half rose from her chair; unexpected company disturbed her and lots of times she went on upstairs, leaving Bill to entertain them himself. Most people apparently realized how she felt and very few came now.

Bill answered the knock, and before Ursula could leave he ushered Paul Mitchell into the room. "You know Mr. Mitchell, don't you, Ursula?" Bill asked.

She said yes, of course, and then they all sat down to what might have been an awkward situation, except that Mitchell remarked casually to Bill, "Somebody told me you played chess and I thought we might have a game."

Bill said yes, he did play, although he hadn't for some little time. He was plainly a little disconcerted at a visitor who would come without invitation and then suggest the manner in which they would spend their time. But he set up the board and the chessmen, and before long the two of them were lost in the game. Ursula watched them and forgot about going up to bed—although neither of them spoke very much, and she thought wryly that for all the entertainment they offered she might as well be at a Quaker meeting! Still, it was pleasant to sit by and watch Bill enjoy himself. She was toying with the idea of going out to the kitchen and making coffee when Mitchell turned to her and said, "Some coffee would really be good now. . . ."

She looked at him in surprise, half suspecting him of

being a mind reader. And if he was all that smart, would he also know why she hesitated? She couldn't bring herself to serve anything to guests in this house—especially coffee—without feeling they were remembering the days when she used to serve them in Martin's Café. But Paul Mitchell couldn't possibly know she'd been a waitress, she reminded herself, and so she went out to the kitchen and came back presently with a tray of cups and a pot of steaming coffee. She found herself enjoying the ritual of serving them and she thought that perhaps she and Bill might have coffee in the den every night after supper.

Mitchell stayed late, and after he was gone she and Bill tidied the room together. When he had put away the chess set, he came out to the kitchen to dry the coffee cups for her and they chatted easily about the evening.

"Cheeky rascal, isn't he?" Bill said. "Just walked in and practically demanded a chess game."

"And ordered coffee like—" She had started to say, like a customer at a restaurant counter, and then she stopped, looking guiltily at Bill and hoping he hadn't noticed her slip.

"As if he were right at home," Bill said. "Guess we should be grateful he didn't ask for steak!"

They both laughed at that. It had been a long time since she and Bill had laughed together.

Later, as they were getting ready for bed, she said,

"I'm glad he came. I enjoyed him."

"Me too," Bill said. "Hope he comes back. It was a nice evening." It was then that she had decided she needed only one sleeping pill.

Now, this morning, she was recalling the evening, analyzing her pleasure. While Paul Mitchell was here, she and Bill had seemed—well, more of a couple.

She had never understood why she should feel guilty about being married to Bill. Certainly he hadn't *had* to marry her.

That phrase, accompanied by knowing looks, had been a part of Ursula's growing up. "She *had* to marry," people would say of some girl or other. And then later, if a baby arrived, there would be the swift calculation on the fingers, the checking of marriage date against birth date. Even before she understood the implication she sensed the shame and disgrace connected with such situations. No, Bill hadn't been forced to marry her.

She thought back over that long-gone summer, glowing once more in its warmth, reliving the time when Bill had loved her—loved her so much and so desperately that he wanted to be with her every minute. At the time it had occurred to her to wonder why his parents didn't interfere —the Thorndykes, who were so sure of themselves and their place in the town. Later she was to find that they were confident nothing would come of Bill's romance. When vacation was over, they reasoned, he would go back to college and this waitress—"Pretty little thing, isn't she! Can't say I blame him"—would settle down to her job at the café once more.

What the Thorndykes had failed to understand was Ursula herself. By nature she was what people described, for want of a better phrase, as "a good girl." Moreover, she was not as unmindful of her extraordinary beauty as it seemed on the surface, although her awareness did not take quite the usual form. As if by instinct, she seemed to see it as a most excellent bargaining device which, if properly employed, would enable her to set her own terms. That those terms meant marriage was nothing to her discredit, for she was not influenced in any way by Bill's position in the town. She loved him deeply, but even so, she wasn't going to let him kiss her on their initial dates. Later, when she began to feel he was really serious, she relented, allowing him two kisses per date, making of the experience a gesture so childlike and innocent that even she was aware of his surprise and delight.

Her reasoning was simple and elemental. If a man really loved a girl, he asked her to marry him. There was no in-between.

And so the situation drifted along. Bill was seemingly more in love with her each day; Ursula was in love too, but also determined to stand firm. Then came the evening in August just a week before Bill was to go back to school. They were out driving in his car and she felt a ripple of uneasiness as he had turned the car into a little-traveled road and stopped under an overhanging tree.

With an urgency both unfamiliar and frightening, he reached across the seat to pull her into his arms. "I can't leave you," he whispered fiercely. "I can't go back to Austin and leave you here, Ursula!"

The way he was holding her and kissing her—well, she knew the situation was getting out of hand. "Bill," she said firmly, "let me go." At the same time she managed to reach behind her and open the car door. The very unexpectedness of her action threw him off guard and he released her. One quick motion and she was out of the car. She turned toward the direction of town and started walking. She had gone only a few steps when his voice came to her.

"Don't be a fool," he said thickly. "Get back in."
She hesitated.

"I'll behave," he told her. "Get back in." A ring of authority was in his voice. "You're five miles from town."
She got back into the car.

"All right," Bill said. He spoke wearily, as if he had fought this thing out and had at last surrendered. "Ursula, let's get married."

She couldn't speak. She sat there stunned and unbelieving.

"All right," he continued, impatient now. "Will you?"

"I—I guess so," she faltered.

He had the grace to laugh then. His voice was shaky, but it was nonetheless a laugh. The sound of it was comforting to her.

"Oh, Bill," she said. "Of course I will. And thank you for asking me."

He kissed her again, and this time she wasn't afraid. He started the car then, and for a moment her fear returned. They weren't headed for town.

"Where are we going?" she asked.

"New Mexico, Miss Scaredy Cat."

"New Mexico?"

"We'll be married over there," he said. "Tonight."

She did not question his statement. Everyone knew that just over the New Mexico line accommodating license clerks could be induced to sell marriage licenses at almost any hour, just as it was common knowledge that there was always a justice of the peace who would perform the ceremony without asking any questions beyond those necessary to make the marriage legal. Lots of couples slipped across the border and came back man and wife. Still, she hesitated.

"Do you think we should? I mean, so fast and everything, without—well, without telling anyone?"

Without telling his parents, she meant.

The Man Who Told the Truth

He did not even answer. His mind made up, he seemed to have a single purpose and determination. The road spread out before them, bright in their headlights, and then retreated darkly as they left it behind. They crossed the state line.

It was strange, she thought now, how little she remembered of her wedding except the unreality of it—appearing before the license clerk who, as it happened, was still in his office because another couple had just been there; then seeking out a justice of the peace.

The justice was a secondhand-store owner who lived in an apartment over his store. The apartment was reached by a very steep outside stairway with a right-angled turn just at the top. Bill and Ursula climbed it, their steps sounding loud in the night. Once inside, Bill spoke to the justice of the peace, and without any more ado the man performed the ceremony, his wife and daughter acting as witnesses.

Bill slipped a plain ring on her finger—she supposed he had bought it from the justice of the peace. Then he kissed her, and she thought: We're married now. It's all right. I'm his wife—always, always. After this, it will be all right. . . .

She was still giddy with the thought and with the great happiness it gave her when they went out the door and started down the steps. She didn't know how it happened

—did one ever know about such things? At any rate, she stumbled or caught her heel, and the next thing she knew she was falling, with Bill trying vainly to grab hold of her—her body rolling down the steep stairway, making the turn at the top, rolling over and over, while Bill ran after her calling "Ursula, Ursula!" his voice full of panic. She fell at last to the concrete walk at the bottom, and then the blackness and the pain closed in on her.

The next thing she remembered was waking up in a hospital bed and crying wildly, "Bill, Bill!"

"He'll be back in a minute," a nurse reassured her. "He's been with you all along, but he's gone for a bite to eat now."

She drifted off again, and when she next awakened Bill was at her side. And standing with him were his parents. It was almost as if she were seeing clearly, and shrinking from, the pattern their relationship was to follow down the years.

On the surface, the elder Thorndykes did more than anyone could have expected of them. Ursula had the best of care—months in the hospital while the doctors pieced her broken body back together. When she was able to leave the hospital the Thorndykes took her to their own house and saw that she had everything she could possibly wish for except the thing she wanted most—their love or, failing that, their respect. This they never saw fit to bestow. Always scrupulously polite, they made little effort to conceal the fact that they considered their son's marriage to Ursula a great tragedy.

There were times when Ursula thought they would have preferred that Bill had merely got her pregnant. Then they would have grounds for despising her. Maybe they even felt that, in such an event they could have bought her off and sent her away somewhere, out of their lives. As it was, she was always before them—Bill's wife, whom he had married of his own free will. In their polite, well-bred way they almost dared the marriage to succeed. And they had gone to their graves resenting her.

She put her hand to the back of her head now. The headache which she had thought she might escape today was returning. She'd stack the dishes for Carmen, the Mexican girl who came each day, and take a pill and go to bed and try to sleep.

Bill Thorndyke unlocked the side door of the bank and walked inside.

"Good morning, Mr. Thorndyke," the janitor said. "Nice day."

"Yes," Bill agreed.

The bank smelled of wax and cleaning agents and sweeping compound. A rather special odor, Bill thought. His father had occasionally mentioned it, saying that he found it pleasant when he opened up mornings.

Jim Carew had held the biggest slice of stock in the bank, but it was W. A. Thorndyke, Bill's father, who had wielded the power. This had been his empire. He had ruled like a benevolent despot over subjects who both loved and respected him. No farmer or rancher ever felt the least hesitancy about coming in wearing his big hat and boots and working clothes, to sit at W. A.'s desk and talk; women trusted him and children gravely discussed their savings accounts with him. He was unfailingly courteous to all of them, and never anything but fair. His father had been a good man, Bill thought, upright and respected.

Bill shifted his thoughts quickly, suddenly conscious of another smell, faint but unmistakable, underlying the wax and soap the janitor had used so lavishly. The front door was open now and the employees were coming in— among them, Shelley Carew. It was her perfume he had smelled, a provocative and unusual scent.

She made her way back to the small room she used as an office, nodding brightly to the janitor and then to Bill. Seeing her, Bill Thorndyke felt a sense of excitement that sent his blood racing through his veins. It was as though he had come alive with her entrance.

And why shouldn't he? He was still young. Why shouldn't he *feel* young at forty-one? he asked himself sharply. He gathered up some papers—none of them of great importance, but any one of them good enough to serve as an excuse—and walked across the lobby to Shelley's office.

Whenever she saw Bill Thorndyke, Shelley Carew thought, Poor guy—he has a pretty thin time of it. People said his wife was practically a case for an institution, and that was what he went home to, night after night. She felt quick sympathy for this good, decent man who through no real fault of his own had missed out on so many of the things other men took for granted.

She also felt a tremendous sense of gratitude toward him. Without Bill Thorndyke's help, she never could have managed to take over as she had done. He was unfailingly kind and understanding, and he knew almost as much about the Carew holdings as her father had known himself. Besides that, he was a bulwark to lean upon when personal problems came up. For instance, others in Benson said, "My goodness, Shelley, we thought you'd bring your mother *home*. You could have a nurse and Cousin Hester with her here just as easily as down there in Dallas." But Bill Thorndyke had told her, "Well, Shelley, you'll have to work things out in the way you think best. That's what your father always did."

Perhaps, she thought, the very limitations of his happi-

ness had given him a deeper understanding and sympathy
than most people had, people whose lives had worked out
more satisfactorily. Maybe suffering did stamp its good
mark on people. Schooled by disappointment and trouble,
as Bill probably was, he might have suspected her real
reason for leaving her mother in Dallas. Mrs. Carew needed
a doctor frequently, and in Benson who was there to call
but Larry Beckwith?

And she would not call Larry Beckwith. She would
not have him think that she was running after him again.
Careful as she was to keep away from him, she knew he
probably believed that even her decision to come to Benson
and look after things was just another maneuver on her
part to get him back.

He could think as he liked. She knew her real reason,
and that was enough. She had to take over the responsibility for her father's estate, complex and intricate though
it was. Her father had built his fortune mostly for her
sake, and she knew it. To him, money had represented
only an exchange value, like the beads the Indians once
used. He had thought of it in terms of what it would
bring—and mostly, what it would bring to her.

"You want that, Baby?" he had asked of all sorts of
things, from mink coats to dime-store knickknacks. "You
want that, Baby? All right, I'll get it for you."

74

And as for Larry Beckwith: "You want him, Baby? All right, I'll get him for you."

Oh, why did she have to keep thinking about Larry? It was some sort of perverseness, like biting on an aching tooth.

Well, her father hadn't got Larry for her. And, what was even worse—and less understandable—she had not got him for herself. Some day she was going to face up to that and explore the reasons.

Now, seeing Bill Thorndyke coming toward her office, she knew she had to take care of this pile of papers on her desk, and the others Bill was bringing to her, and all those others that would be waiting for her when she went back to Dallas tomorrow. For she was looking after her father's affairs, rather than hiring a manager, because it made her feel she was at last showing some sort of appreciation for him. Had she allowed someone else to take over, it would have been like saying that the far-flung business empire Jim Carew had spent his life building was not worthy of her attention. In the last months before her father's death, he had seemed to feel this was her attitude, without ever actually accusing her. And he had blamed himself for it, which she found difficult to understand.

When she told him that Larry had broken off their engagement, just when he was nearly finished with his internship and they could be married, her father was furious. "He can't do it to you, Baby! Men don't break engagements."

"He did."

"I'm going to have a talk with that young buck!"

Her father was halfway to the door before she stopped him. "No!" she cried, holding to his arm. "You can't!"

"I'd like to know why." His face was an angry crimson, his breathing heavy.

"Because—" She sought for some words that would quiet him, keep him from doing this impossible thing he threatened. "Because I don't want him, that's why. I told him so."

Her father hesitated, visibly torn between the suspicion that she was lying and the thought that he could make himself ridiculous in what might well be interpreted as the father-with-a-shotgun act.

"It's all my fault, Baby," he said, sitting down wearily. "But of course, if you don't want him . . ."

"Well, I don't," she said firmly. "Now, let's talk about something else."

"Like maybe . . ." He fumbled for an idea, looking hopefully at her, wanting to hit on something that would give her pleasure. "Like, well—a long cruise? Your mother and you and I?"

He made the suggestion with a tentative, upward inflection in his voice.

Why not? The quicker she got away from here, and the farther, the better it suited her.

"That sounds wonderful," she said.

They went on the trip, but none of them enjoyed it very much. Shelley was in no frame of mind to enjoy anything. Her father, for some reason she did not understand, acted as if the broken engagement had been all his fault. She would never cease believing that the nagging worry on his part was the real cause of the heart attack he had had on their way home.

So in a way she had been responsible for his death, and now the least she could do was to make herself personally responsible for the inheritance he had left her. To do less would have constituted, in her own mind at least, a repudiation of her father and all the hopes he had had for her.

Bill Thorndyke entered her office just at that moment and she looked up to say, "Good morning."

- 5 -

MUCH TO BEN LANGLEY'S DISGUST, THE FINE WEATHER CON-
tinued. So long as the sun shone every day, mothers went
on letting their kids wear summer clothes, and that was
that. People were a lot like the grasshopper in the fable;
in warm weather they couldn't believe winter would ever
come.

"Why don't you put on a sale?" Paul Mitchell suggested one day.

A sale in October? Ben Langley had never heard of
such a thing and said so. Sales came in August, when the
mothers were supposed to buy school clothes (although
usually they didn't), and again in January, when all the
white goods were marked down.

"You don't have to go on doing things the way you
always did just because you always did them that way,"
Paul Mitchell remarked mildly.

Ben Langley frowned. Who was this young whippersnapper, to tell him what to do? Probably wanting to get his hands on things and run the store for himself!

But Mitchell's face was bland as cream, and something about his detachment served to calm Langley. Instead of answering hotly, as he had meant to do, Ben caught himself looking around the store. In spite of himself, he saw a lot of items—those boys' slacks, for instance, and some girls' sweaters that hadn't sold as well as he had expected them to.

Then he heard himself saying, "Okay. Let's look around and check a few items that it might be well to move. Not everything, mind you . . ."

And again, he had a strange feeling that his words came as a complete surprise to his clerk.

"Oh," Paul Mitchell said, at once alert and interested, "so you plan to have some specials? That's a good idea, with business as slow as it is now."

It proved to be an excellent idea. Before the sale was over, Ben Langley had added a number of items he had never meant to include in the first place, and the cash registers worked overtime, even with the weather still acting as though it were summer.

Martha Donnell, sitting idly at her desk now that the last student had gone, sighed and decided she, too, had had enough of the unseasonably warm weather. The children were restless, her feet hurt, and before the day was half over she was worn out. Part of it, she decided, could be that she wasn't making out as well with Clark as she might have wished—tender loving care notwithstanding.

She did everything she could for him at home, but he still didn't like school. Poor kid—he didn't know the first thing in the world about getting along with other children and he was frightened of his teacher, Mrs. Bellamy (too bad he had to draw *her*, Martha thought; just a year short of retirement age, Mrs. Bellamy had never possessed either great patience or any special love for her young charges). In spite of all Martha could do, Clark seemed ready to withdraw into his own private world to insulate himself against shock and hurt.

The second day of school Clark had come in to say he didn't like it and did he have to go back, and Martha had said of course he did—everyone went to school. The third morning he had said he was sick, and he looked it, so she called Mrs. Beckwith to come stay with him. And then she had a talk with Mrs. Bellamy, which helped a little but not much. That was just about the way things stood now—a little better but not much.

Looking back now, she realized she had been quite smug in her confidence that she could do a great deal for her nephew.

She should go home now and check with him to see

80

how the day had gone, although she felt in advance that it had been far from good. Maybe if she cooked something special for him it would help. Actually, she felt too tired either to shop for groceries or to cook, and she was tempted to go to Daisy Higdon's for supper this evening. It wasn't much more expensive than cooking in.

At home she found Clark inside the house instead of playing outdoors in the fine weather. The TV was going at top volume, blaring out a Western. She hated to tell the boy to turn it down, but she thought it would drive her wild if it went on. So she took the indirect approach.

"Go wash your face and comb your hair and put on a clean shirt," she told him. "We're going to Mrs. Hidgon's for supper."

He looked mildly pleased at the idea, but amazed her by saying, "*You* aren't."

"Oh, I'm going too," she told him.

"I mean, *you* aren't combing your hair and changing your clothes."

She thought, Why not? So she decided to take a bath and change her dress and redo her hair.

They were a little late; Mrs. Higdon was just announcing the meal when they walked in.

"You sit here, next to Mr. Mitchell," Daisy told Clark.

The man shot a startled look at the boy. For one quick instant, Martha thought he was going to get up and move.

"If Mr. Mitchell doesn't mind," Martha put in hastily. Lone men sometimes were finicky about having small boys sit next to them at the table.

Paul Mitchell seemed to come back from a great distance. "Of course I don't mind," he said amiably. "Sit down. Your name is Clark, isn't it?"

Good heavens! Martha thought. Asking Clark's name after all the times they had talked together! Surely he couldn't have forgotten the many evenings he had spent on the Donnell front porch.

"You know it is," Clark told him calmly, taking his seat beside Paul Mitchell.

The meal went off pleasantly enough. Clark's table manners were good. Martha, sitting across from him, decided there was no reason they shouldn't come here often instead of thinking it was a treat reserved only for Sundays. Paul Mitchell, after his strange behavior at first, began talking in an animated way. In the midst of the meal a candle fly, much to Daisy Higdon's embarrassment, invaded the dining room. As if by design, the insect made a dive directly at Clark. The boy dodged, almost upsetting his milk.

"Well," Mitchell said, "you need to be a boxer to handle that fellow."

"What's a boxer?" Clark asked.

Mitchell looked startled, as if he wondered where the

boy had been keeping himself, but all he said was, "I'll show you after you've finished eating."

When dinner was over he and Clark went outside by themselves, and Martha could hear snatches of Mitchell's instructions to the boy. She sat chatting with the other boarders, feeling comfortable and free with no dishes to wash and Clark outdoors having a good time.

Finally she stood up, and with no great urge to follow her own direction, said it was time to take Clark home and put him to bed. Outside she saw Larry Beckwith walking by, looking a little tired. For a moment he hesitated in front of the boardinghouse and she gazed at him, wishing she could do something to erase those lines of fatigue. But only Shelley Carew had the power to do that.

Larry paused a moment, as if half considering coming in. Then he seemed to think better of it and walked on toward the Beckwith house, which stood dark and lonely a block down the street.

In the side yard Martha saw that Paul Mitchell had recruited another boy, who was about Clark's size—a newcomer to the neighborhood whom Martha knew only as Jock—and had the two boys sparring away at each other with great enthusiasm. Noting with pleasure that Clark wasn't doing badly, she turned back into Mrs. Higdon's. She'd stay just a while longer. This was better for him than getting to bed on time.

Larry Beckwith was indeed tired. He had stayed later than he had anticipated at Miss Stacie's library, going by at her request. It seemed that she wanted to check with him about Paul Mitchell.

"Do you know anything about him?" Miss Stacie had asked. "A single, solitary thing? He comes to the library a lot, and I sort of wonder."

"If you mean have I seen his birth certificate or his social security card," Larry told her, "the answer is no. But I suspect Ben Langley has that information."

"Well, that's not exactly what I had in mind," she said. "It's more what a doctor would notice—the way he seems to go off into a trance sometimes, and then wakes up and says and does the strangest things."

"Like what?" Larry asked, regarding her keenly.

"Like, well . . ." Miss Stacie blushed a little, looked as if she didn't want to go on, and then laughed ruefully. "Well—like yesterday, for instance. He came in after supper—I stay open evenings, you know. There were some kids in here fooling around, making a lot of noise and that sort of thing. So I just went over to them—they were sitting at the table next to Mr. Mitchell—and I told them to hush up or get out."

"That's nothing unusual," Larry said with a laugh. "You've told me that upon occasion."

84

Miss Stacie seemed not to notice his interruption. "I said they weren't going to act like that in my library," she went on. "And do you know what he—that Paul Mitchell—said to me? Right out of a blue sky?"

"I can't imagine. Tell me."

"He said—" she began, and then stopped, looking embarrassed. "He said, sort of faraway-like, as if he were thinking out loud, 'I thought this was a *public* library.' That's what he said."

Larry threw back his head and laughed. In the old days, Miss Stacie would have thrown him out for less.

"Stop laughing, Larry," Miss Stacie said seriously. "I haven't been able to laugh myself and I won't have you doing it. I've been thinking. Do I act as if this library is mine? I mean, am I obnoxious about it?"

Instantly he was sober. "It *is* your library, Miss Stacie. You've given your life to it."

"That's not what I mean," she told him brusquely, "and you know it. I want you to tell me if I had it coming. Because if so, I'll try to change my ways. I won't promise to do it, but I can try."

He considered the matter gravely, knowing this was no time for a light, quick reply. Miss Stacie had been hurt, as much as his mother would have been had someone questioned her method of rearing her son. And, unbidden, the whole problem of Paul Mitchell came back to him. Miss Stacie wasn't the only one in town who had received a few blunt words from him. Everyone was still smiling about the way he had got Ben Langley to put on a sale, Ben having inadvertently dropped the information himself after the sale turned out so well. And there were other instances. Not even he himself had escaped. No more than a week ago Mitchell had looked straight at him and said, "You don't *have* to be a specialist, you know. We need general practitioners more than any other sort of doctor right now." Larry had reddened in embarrassment. He hadn't as yet—probably wouldn't for a long time—got over regretting that he couldn't go on for three years of specialization before he started practicing. How could Paul Mitchell have guessed that?

Miss Stacie's question, honestly put, deserved an honest answer. The only trouble was that he was puzzled himself. Might as well be honest—Miss Stacie would catch on anyway.

"If I had ever brought myself to believe in extrasensory perception—which I have not," he told her, "I'd say Mitchell had it. He seems to go around reading our minds and then forgetting what he's read." He looked at her hopefully. "You have an idea?" he asked.

"Well, not exactly. But 'there are more things in heaven and earth, Horatio, than are dreamt of in your philosophy,' " she quoted glibly. "Or mine either, as far as that goes," she added.

He grinned at her. Miss Stacie was quite a girl. He'd never forget how she used to handle his overdue fines. Not that she forgave them—not Miss Stacie. That would have been in violation of her sense of responsibility to the library. She had a different system.

"You can shovel the snow off the walk," she would say. Or, if there was no snow, he could mow the yard, or go to the post office for her, or help with rebinding. He had never felt as if he were accepting charity. Around her, he considered himself adult and able to work out his own problems. What if she did do a lot of talking about what went on in town? She was never vindictive or cruel. Maybe it kept a lot of people walking straighter, knowing that if they stepped aside Miss Stacie would spread the news. Maybe every town needed a built-in conscience equipped with a loud-speaker.

Anyway, he wasn't going to let the chance words of a stranger hurt Miss Stacie, who was as good as gold.

"Don't you give him a thought," he told her now. "Just go on running your library and be proud that's the way we all think of it. Paul Mitchell's an outsider. You can't expect him to understand our ways."

"Maybe," Miss Stacie said with a sniff, "he understands them all the better for being an outsider."

"Well, forget about him, anyway," he advised her. "And now I'd better be getting along home."

"Get along with you," Miss Stacie said. "And if ever I have an ache—God forbid—I promise to come see you and not drive over to Medalia to the clinic."

Larry gave her a sharp look and then decided it was just one of Miss Stacie's jokes.

"Call me any time you need me," he told her.

He walked out into the street, almost deserted now. In Benson people went home for supper, and that was what they called it. The few people eating in Martin's Café looked dejected and alone, as if even life itself had cast them off, sentencing them to that worst of all fates, being stranded in Benson and eating at a café. He averted his eyes from the sight as he walked by. It was late, and his mother was away overnight on a nursing case. He'd stop and see if Daisy Higdon could feed him.

He should be going to a home of his own, he thought. Really his own. Maybe a jerry-built house in a new development, but his own. And there should be a wife waiting for him. Not just any wife—Shelley should be there.

He let the twisting bitterness of such thoughts wash over him as seldom as he could. Usually he had to keep his mind on his patients. But there was no denying the memory that came to him now. It was as poignant and as disturbing as the day it had happened.

The Man Who Told the Truth

He was graduated from medical school, not at the top of his class but close enough. He was conscious of the solemnity of the occasion—the binding oath he took and the meaning of it, a significance far beyond the power of the layman to understand. Maybe his mother understood a little as she sat there in the front row with Shelley Carew at her side; next to Shelley sat Jim Carew and Mrs. Carew. His mother touched her eyes with her gloved finger and he knew, even though he saw the gesture out of the corner of his eye, that she was crying. He could see that Shelley too was wiping her eyes, and on her face was a look of pride and love. Mr. Carew himself was deeply moved, although his joy came from seeing Shelley's happiness. Even so, Larry's heart reached out to them, the people who loved him. Their joy became the focal point of his consciousness, lifting the moment of his graduation to an experience far above the mere personal triumph of having at last achieved his ambition.

They all had dinner together that evening. Jim Carew took them to the Martinique, and to give him credit, he did the whole thing in the best of taste. Nobody could say here was a rich Texas rancher come to town to make a show of himself. Larry liked the way his mother looked, in a simple dress that was pretty and tasteful, even though he realized it had probably been bought at Ben Langley's on sale. Mrs. Carew, as usual, was not quite holding together, with a few strands of her hair loose and her dress a bit too fussy. But then, he had to remember she was at least twenty years older than his mother.

Shelley, of course, was exactly right, as always. He couldn't have described what she wore, but he knew it was perfect for her. This year when all the other girls were wearing their hair short, hers was long and done up in a sleek, smooth twist in back. She didn't even seem to notice that people turned to look at her. There was a glow about her, and yet a certain softness, too. He felt his pulses stir at the sight of her.

Mr. Carew broke in on his thoughts to say, "Well, I think if you have all had enough, Mama and Mrs. Beckwith and I will go back to the hotel. It's been a long day. You kids can drop us off."

At the car, he handed Larry the keys. "Here, you drive, boy. You know this town better than I do."

Larry slipped in behind the wheel of the Cadillac, feeling a certain exaltation as the powerful motor started, and at the same time a sense of embarrassment at driving this car. It wasn't just any car—it was Jim Carew's. And so it was therefore Shelley's, like all Jim's possessions. If he just weren't so obvious about the whole thing . . .

The Carews and his mother got out at the hotel, and then, as if the whole thing had been prearranged, he and Shelley drove off. She did not suggest where they might go, leaving the decision to him. He found himself driving down Lake Road and, ultimately, down a lane lined with trees. Once there, he stopped the car and took Shelley in his arms.

She was very sweet; she was wonderful. He ought to be able to think of a better way to say it. "Shelley," he whispered, and it sounded like a word new-coined to tell his love for her. Against his ear Shelley was saying, "Larry, darling . . ."

He came back from a great distance to realize that she was speaking again. "Larry," she said, "oh, Larry, let's get married right away."

"Uh-huh," he said, not wanting to talk, attempting to pull her back into his arms again.

"I mean while we're down here. Dad said he'd send us to Acapulco on our honeymoon."

He jerked away from her, dismay and even anger rising in him. Afterward he thought that perhaps the sudden shock of returning to sordid reality was too much for him. Why else should he have answered so quickly, so rudely?

"Listen, Shelley, I have a year of internship ahead of me. And then three years of residency, if I expect to have any kind of decent practice."

"You mean," she said, her voice cold and level—like, he thought, Old Man Carew sizing up a sorry herd someone was trying to pass off on him—"you mean you don't intend to marry for another four years?"

"Well, one at least," he told her lamely. It did sound insane, when you thought about it, to love each other as much and as long as he and Shelley had and then say marriage had to wait.

"An intern has very little more money than a med student," he pointed out sensibly.

"Silly," she said. "Silly, to talk about money. You know Dad wants to—"

"You know I can't let your father support us, Shelley."

"I don't see why. If he wants to. And *I* want to . . . After all," she reminded him, "we've been engaged—well, sort of—for four years!"

She leaned toward him, her face tilted upward. He turned away. And that was how the quarrel started.

It was the first time he had ever seen her really angry. Something of Jim Carew was in her towering rage, plus a quality all her own. He himself put on a fairly good exhibition too. He could not recall all that was said—there was too much and it was too bitter—but he knew quite well how it ended. She told him to change places with her—she wanted to go back to the hotel, and she'd drive the car herself. He flung open his door—it was a wonder he didn't rip it off the hinges—and said for her to take over. He didn't want to drive Jim Carew's car anyway, and he'd be damned if he'd go on acting like a kept man. The last was said over his shoulder, for he had started walking toward town.

Even in his rage he managed a bitter grin. This was a switch, all right. Boy walks home!

"Larry!" He heard her imperious cry, but he only walked faster. She called again.

He did not turn or even hesitate. Behind him he heard the car turn around, and he looked back to see that she was coming down the road toward him. Mad as she was, he wouldn't have been surprised if she had tried to run him down. But the car drew up beside him and he heard her say, gently this time, "Larry, please."

He stopped, halted more by the gentleness in her voice than he would ever have been by her commands.

"I'm sorry," she said gently. She could see he was weakening—she was the discerning one. "Get back in the car. Please . . ."

When he hesitated, she went on: "I *said* I was sorry." Impatience edged her voice. She seemed to imply: What do you expect me to do? Get down and grovel? If she had said it, he would have walked on, but he happened to look at her. She was crying.

That did it. He opened the car door. "Idiot," he said. "Here, move over."

She did, and he got into the driver's seat. Then he bent to kiss her—gently this time, something giving way in his heart as he did so. Briefly the knowledge came to him that

Shelley was very vulnerable and young, and it was up to him to be the adult in this situation. He would handle things from here on out and call the shots, and it was time she realized it.

"Shelley," he told her, "now you listen to me. I love you and I want to marry you. But not until I can support you. Understand?"

She said nothing.

"Do you understand?"

"Yes," she said softly. And then, "That's almost the first time you said it."

"Said what?"

"That you loved me."

"Well, I do and I have—a long time. And you know it —you've known it all along. So let's stop bickering, and you quit trying to run things. Hear me? Because I don't intend to get married until I can take care of you."

Again there was a long pause. Finally, when she did answer it was the old Shelley once more—indomitable, a little mocking. But sweet—all the sweeter for the hint of irony beneath her words.

"All right, have things your way. Though just for your information, it's the girl who is supposed to set the day."

They both laughed then and suddenly things were all right between them. He kissed her again, thinking as he did so that he had never before loved her so much. . . .

The memory of that night was so bright and clear **now**, as he walked down the street in Benson, that he found **he** had gone past Mrs. Higdon's house. Oh, well, he **really** wasn't very hungry. He would go home and see what **his** mother had left in the refrigerator. Half a block down **he** could see the Carew house, dark now except for a light **in** the caretaker's quarters. That meant Shelley had gone **back** to Dallas. Her presence had been so real to him that, as **he** turned in at his own gate, it seemed almost as if the **ghost** of a little girl ran after him calling, "Larry, wait a **minute!** I'm coming. . . ."

- 6 -

BILL THORNDYKE SLIPPED INTO A VACANT CHAIR AT THE MEN'S
Civic Club luncheon. He was a little late and the singing
had already started—preceded, no doubt, by the usual horse-
play in which the members felt they must engage in order
to prove they were having a good time. Usually the songs
were mere continuations of the clowning, especially since
Ben Langley had been elected song leader. Langley had a
voice like an asthmatic bullfrog and the job had been given
him in the same spirit that moves small boys to call their
fat comrade "Skinny."

Ben begrudged the time it took to come to the basement of the Methodist Church each Wednesday for the
club luncheons. Today, apparently, he had rebelled and
sent his clerk, Paul Mitchell, in his place. Bill Thorndyke
slipped into his chair just as Mitchell was saying, "All
right, fellows, start over. And by the way, whoever told
you it was smart to murder a song?"

Bill, watching the men's faces grow sober, grinned a little. They looked for all the world like small boys taking a scolding they knew they deserved. But they were not resentful. It was amazing how Mitchell went around town telling people plain truths about themselves. Nobody else could have got by with it. Perhaps the secret lay in the way he did it— in a completely detached and impersonal manner.

"Start over," Mitchell was saying now, nodding to Martha Donnell at the piano. She was really a rather good-looking girl, Bill Thorndyke reflected. A little prim, with her long hair and neatly tailored dresses, but pretty anyway. Too bad she always had someone around her neck—parents, brother and now her nephew. She would have made some man a wonderful wife. She had a sense of humor and a way with children. She looked especially nice today, animated and gay. Even as he reflected briefly on the unfairness of life, Martha struck up "Home on the Range." Directed by Mitchell, the men gave a not-too-bad rendition of the song.

Membership in the Civic Club was a duty inherited by Bill from his father—along with the job at the bank, the house he and Ursula lived in, and the knowledge that he must always be a leader and a man of unimpeachable rectitude. Automatically, whether he wanted these things or not, they came to him.

And they seemed impossible for him to escape. For instance, why had they continued to live in the big house? Bill had no fondness for it and Ursula had never liked it. For her, he was sure, it was always associated with the difficult months of recovery from her accident. At his mother's insistence she had been brought there when she was able to leave the hospital and installed in an upstairs bedroom with a private nurse skilled in physical therapy. Ursula had to learn to walk all over again—a feat she might never have accomplished, he sometimes thought, if he had not been drafted about that time. He was sent to Florida, and she was so determined to join him that she made herself walk—willed it, almost, just in order to be out of that house! And she had succeeded, in spite of several doctors saying she'd never be able to do it.

He supposed that the Florida interval had been the happiest in their lives. They had had an apartment, and loved the easy, informal way of life Florida offered them. There they had captured some of their old relationship.

The war ended before he was sent overseas, and Bill had scarcely been mustered out when his father died. They moved in with his mother—there didn't seem any way out of it. Mrs. Thorndyke was all alone in the big house, and not strong, and terribly insistent that they come. Of course, Ursula did not want to do this, nor, as a matter of fact, did Bill. But both of them realized that in the eyes of everyone in Benson, any other arrangement would be unthinkable.

They had hardly settled themselves when Ursula's headaches started. When Bill's mother died, four years later, the headaches had become a seemingly inescapable part of the young Thorndykes' lives. No two doctors agreed on the reason for them; only one offered any semblance of relief, and that was old Dr. Grayson with his pills. Bill hated to think what would happen if he couldn't get them for her. Her life had narrowed down so much that the pills were about all she asked of it.

She shrank from meeting new people; always she shied away from those who were anything but careful and considerate in their treatment of her. She wouldn't go into the library because Miss Stacie was so brusque. She went to Dr. Larry Beckwith once and wouldn't go back because, after giving her a thorough examination, he said, "Honestly, Mrs. Thorndyke, I can't find anything organically wrong with you. You're a bit nervous and run-down, but it's nothing to be alarmed about."

She said later that Larry Beckwith was too young to be a doctor and didn't put his mind on his patient. And she never went back.

But oddly enough she liked Paul Mitchell. The man had started dropping in now and then. He never called ahead of time, just knocked on the door and smiled ingratiatingly when Bill opened it. "Thought I'd come by and see if you wanted to play chess."

So they played chess, with Ursula sitting by watching. The first time she broke in on their silent contemplation of the chessboard, Mitchell turned to her and said, quietly but with authority, that watchers didn't interrupt players. Why didn't she get some knitting or something to occupy her while she watched?

Ursula drew back, tears coming into her eyes, deeply hurt that he should have spoken so abruptly to her. Bill braced himself for a scene, but even as he did so, Paul Mitchell spoke again, casually.

"You'd enjoy knitting," he said. "Come down to the store and I'll help you pick out some yarn and needles."

"I don't know how to knit," Ursula said.

"I'll teach you," Mitchell told her.

"You know how?" Ursula was lost in wonder, as much at his knowledge as at his offer to teach her.

"Yes, I learned once when I was—" Mitchell broke off abruptly. "Never mind—just come down and we'll start you."

Amazingly enough, Ursula did go, coming back with quantities of bright yarn, some needles, and the pattern for an afghan.

"It's not hard at all," she assured Bill, her face bright

with interest and pleasure at her accomplishment.

After that she knitted whenever the headaches were not bedeviling her—which, Bill reflected, was rather often of late. It was pleasant to hear the click of her needles as he and Mitchell played chess. She had even taken to knitting during the evenings when they were alone, instead of automatically turning on the television.

All in all, Bill reflected as he sat at the Civic Club watching Mitchell conduct the singing, he had reason to be rather grateful to the man. He wished idly that he knew a little more about him.

It was odd about small towns. They could be the nosiest places in the world, but on the other hand they could also accept a man on short notice. Benson had buzzed with talk when Mitchell first came, Bill reflected, but when the man began staying at Daisy Higdon's, working at Langley's, going to Miss Stacie's library and attending the Methodist Church, people accepted him as one of them. Of course, these things had not stopped the talk entirely. Anyone who came up with additional information felt it was his duty to pass it along, and so gradually the townspeople had come to know that Mitchell had grown up in Tennessee, attended Vanderbilt, and had come here from a town in Kansas, where he had worked in a store.

That still left a good many things unexplained. The scar, for instance. When someone asked him about it, he ran his hand over it vaguely and said, "Oh, that?" and changed the subject. Larry Beckwith, when pressed for an opinion, said it looked comparatively recent—maybe a year or two—and there was no way of telling how it got there. An automobile accident, or any one of a dozen ways.

Just as everyone had failed to find out about the origin of the scar, nobody had been able to learn what Mitchell had done with himself in those years between his graduation from Vanderbilt and the job in Kansas. Being an ordinary dry goods clerk seemed rather a—well, a comedown for a college graduate. Maybe that was why he didn't want to discuss the matter.

"That's enough," Mitchell was saying to the club members now, already leafing through their books in anticipation of another song. "No use to overdo. Besides, I think Miss Donnell is going to play us a special number."

Martha swung into a sprightly tune Bill did not recognize, and Paul Mitchell watched her, looking unusually relaxed and happy. Maybe that comes of having licked the pants off me at chess last night, Bill thought. It had been a good evening all around. Ursula had made coffee and served it with pie—bakery pie, but still good. They had sat until nearly midnight, eating and talking, with Ursula acting as if she were thoroughly enjoying herself. Seeing her so delighted at playing hostess, Bill had been strangely touched and wanted to tell her how well she had done.

The Man Who Told the Truth

The desire to congratulate her was still with him when Paul left. As soon as they were alone, Bill reached out to take her hand. It was almost an automatic gesture on his part, but she responded out of all proportion.

"Oh, Bill," she cried, "thank you!"

"What for?" he asked in bewilderment.

"For being so sweet to me."

She clung to him, and he patted her shoulder gently. What else could he do? She slipped her arms around his neck, as shyly as if they had just been married, and he kissed her. Except for cursory pecks, it was the first time he had kissed her for a long, long time.

Martha Donnell decided that since she was already dressed up, she and Clark might as well eat at Daisy Higdon's again this evening. She knew she was spoiling herself, going there so often, but once more wouldn't hurt. It had given her a fine, careless feeling that day at noon to walk out of the school knowing that her lunchroom duties would be looked after, since by playing the piano for the Civic Club she was doing good public relations for the school.

When she arrived at the luncheon she was surprised to find that Paul Mitchell was going to lead the singing. They had a few moments of conference before the songs started, and it struck her that he was unusually animated today and really quite good-looking. She had already decided he was kind and intelligent, but she had never thought him especially handsome. Today there was a vitality about him, an air of authority. From where she sat she could see the long red scar behind his ear, but even that did not detract from his good looks. He smiled at her just before the songs started, and she smiled back. The look was a warm bond between them.

It was very pleasant to be linked thus with him, and even as the thought crossed her mind he looked directly at her again, giving her the strange sensation that he knew exactly what she was thinking. She found herself blushing like a schoolgirl and hoped he didn't know the reason.

All in all, the Civic Club meeting turned out to be fun, and her relaxed, happy mood stayed with her even after she went back to her class. Now, back home once more, she was loath to put an end to the day. She *would* go to Daisy's for supper, she decided. Clark always enjoyed going, and that in itself was reason enough.

The evening at Daisy's turned out to be one of her best. Paul Mitchell, in a talkative mood—perhaps still in a good humor after his success as a song leader—entertained everyone with some stories about a load of gypsies who had come into the store only that day and almost given Ben Langley apoplexy, for fear they might make off with some merchandise—or worse, ask to try something on. Mitchell had a gift for mimicry and everyone at the table laughed at his imitation of his overcautious employer.

When supper was over Clark went over to Mitchell's side and stood regarding him with great interest. Martha struggled with the idea of asking Mitchell to walk home with them and then discarded it. The town would be buzzing its head off before morning. It was all right if he just dropped by, but to ask him . . .

For the second time that day she had the eerie feeling he had read her mind, for he fell into step with her and Clark as they walked out the door. She was conscious of the knowing looks of the other boarders as they went down the street toward her house. At the gate she assumed he would come in, but all he did was to say, "Well, I'll see you again tomorrow, maybe."

She went up the steps to her own house with a sharp sense of disappointment.

"Why didn't he come in with us?" Clark asked. "Why, Aunt Martha?"

"I don't know," she said, her voice sounding a little waspish even in her own ears. The boy looked at her, startled, and then drew back within himself.

"Honey," she said, "he probably had already promised to go somewhere else. Come on—we'll make some taffy!"

The candy was off the stove, out on the back porch cooling, when a knock came at the front door. Martha, thinking it was a neighbor or the paper boy, went to answer it, and there was Paul Mitchell.

"Oh, dear!" she exclaimed. And then, remembering her manners, she said, "Won't you come in?"

"Thank you," he said, and walked inside.

"We were making candy," she told him all in a rush, as if that explained the untidy kitchen, plainly visible from where he stood, and her own confusion as well. "I'm sorry things are in such a mess."

"It looks very nice to me," he said absently. "I'm the one who should apologize, for dropping by like this. I went to the Thorndykes' to play chess, but Bill wasn't home. So I just decided to see you. I hope it's all right."

Her embarrassment had communicated itself to him now, and Martha instantly forgot her own nervousness in trying to put him at ease.

"Will you stay and help Clark and me pull taffy?" she asked. "It should be ready about now."

"Fine. I used to be an expert at it," he told her, smiling warmly. "Just lead me to it."

Shelley Carew, driving her sleek, low-slung foreign car past the library, saw Larry Beckwith walk inside. Darn him, she thought. Now I won't be able to get him out of my mind all the way to Dallas, and I'll probably drive too fast and have half the cops in Texas trailing me.

But running away, she told herself, was not only silly

but useless. She had tried it once—when she had gone on the long cruise—but it had not helped at all. Hurt and despair had been with her all the way. Even now it brought tears to her eyes to recall that trip her father had arranged in order to help her forget Larry Beckwith, whose crazy, lopsided pride forbade their marriage because she happened to have some money.

The whole business didn't make sense. They had things worked out between them—or at least she thought they had —and then, bang! Just when their marriage seemed possible at last, Larry blew up and put an end to everything. She had never been able to sort out in logical sequence the details of that final scene, but the end was conclusive enough. Larry said they weren't going to be married. And wasn't that a switch? she thought wryly—the girl getting the "Dear John" routine.

After he had stormed out of the house that day she thought of many things she could have said to him—that his attitude was simply snobbery in reverse; that she didn't have any more money now than when they had become engaged; that if she didn't mind, he shouldn't. But she never quite got the words out. From the moment he rushed in to tell her, without warning, that the engagement was off, he gave her no chance to talk. Usually as solid as a rock, he behaved as if some great catastrophe had only a moment before landed squarely upon him. What was even more surprising, he acted as if she knew what had upset him and that therefore there was no need for explanation.

He just assumed I'd understand why he was walking out, she thought.

Well, perhaps she did: he didn't love her. If he had, her money wouldn't have made any difference. He had simply used it as an excuse.

But why hadn't he said so?

Yet even here the answer seemed plain enough. He was afraid she wouldn't take his decision as final. He had told her to stay home when she followed him around his paper route, and she had gone right on trailing him. When she was fifteen she had announced that she was going to marry him. All through the years she had run after him, openly and without shame. Naturally, when he wanted to break off, he felt he must do so in such a way as to leave no doubt in her mind about the decision.

Larry didn't love her—apparently never had. He had been kind and thoughtful to the little girl who trailed after him, and she had mistaken his generosity for love. It was this thought with which she tortured herself over all those miles she and her parents had traveled on the cruise. Even so, each time they checked in at a hotel she snatched at the pile of mail waiting for them, hoping against all sense and reason that there would be a letter from Larry.

Always there was the sick, brackish feeling when she

saw there was none. Stacks of mail, but not one piece with meaning for her. She could feel her father's eyes on her, his sensing her hurt and knowing the reason for it. Even her mother, for all her vagueness, probably knew. Shelley, seeing their concern, tried to be very gay; she succeeded in fooling her mother only a little, her father not at all.

It was that way all through the trip. Her father had never once mentioned Larry Beckwith by name, but instead tried in his kindly, bumbling way to help her. Once he handed her, without a word, a bit of advice taken from a lovelorn column, which said that the pain of being jilted should last—for the ordinary run of young girls—no more than six months. By that time she should be well on the way to finding herself another love.

Shelley read it without comment. How could she make her father, or anyone else, understand that she was not the "ordinary run of young girls." Child of an ailing mother and a doting father, both of them nearer the age of grandparents than parents, brought up as an only child without much contact with children of her own age, she couldn't be expected to have the ordinary outlook on things. For instance, she felt that a girl who could make such a swift switch in her affections was in love with love rather than with a specific man. Anyway, she was too much like her father—stubbornly loyal, completely single-minded in his affections—to jump lightly from love to love.

The situation and her reaction to it were put into words one day when, at teatime on the ship coming home, she opened a fortune cooky and read its verse: "You were meant to love one man all your life."

She was seized with a convenient fit of coughing, excused herself and went to her cabin. Once there, she threw herself face down on the bed and cried, a thing she so seldom did.

It was stupid of her, and childish, to blame herself for her father's death. The doctors had warned him that he had a heart condition. Yet there was no denying that his worry over her hurt, combined with the strenuous trip—taken because of her—may have brought on the attack that took his life in San Francisco, just when they were so close to the town he loved.

She had surprised Bill Thorndyke when she announced she was going to look after the business of the estate herself.

"It's quite a job," he had warned her. "Your father never talked much about it, but he has—had—a considerable estate. Ranch and oil and farm lands, bank stock, other financial interests."

"I'd like to try, anyway."

"You're pretty young," he continued, still doubtful.

"I've been very close to my father," she said, not blurting out the truth of her age. Let him come to his own conclusions, or if he must have day, year, and hour, go ask

Miss Stacie, who kept up with such things. "I think I know pretty much what his intent would have been, where it is not clearly stated."

That had seemed to convince Bill Thorndyke.

"All right, Shelley," he said. "Perhaps it is best that way. I'll help you all I can with such business as the bank is concerned with, and you can consult lawyers when you feel the need. The Dallas part will be easier—it's more of a piece."

The Dallas part would be easier, but not for the reason he gave. In Dallas she would have no thought of seeing Larry Beckwith.

Since her father's funeral, when Larry greeted her with the formality he might have used toward a slight acquaintance and extended the customary sympathy, she had scarcely seen him at all except at a distance. She had to assume that he was purposely trying to avoid her.

He had not seen her this afternoon, though, as he went up the steps of the library. Her heart went with him up those steps. Had she followed her own instincts, she would have stopped the car, got out and run after him, calling that old, childish command, "Wait for me, Larry! I'm coming!" If she had, would he have waited, as he used to?

- 7 -

URSULA THORNDYKE LET HERSELF INTO THE HOUSE, A LOOK OF incredulous wonder and delight on her face. She simply couldn't believe it, even after Dr. Larry had told her so. Why had she ever thought he wasn't a good doctor!

She looked at herself in the mirror over the mantel. She thought: I'm pretty again. I'm young. I'm alive.

She had no headache. No headache at all. And she knew she would never again have another one, not as long as she lived. Almost without being conscious of her actions, she went to her bedroom. Once there, she pulled out the drawer of her dressing table with such haste that the contents spilled on the floor. Her pills rolled every which way. Out of habit she stopped to pick them up carefully, one at a time. And then, suddenly, she began grabbing them up by the handful, emptying them into the wastebasket. That was the place for them. Dr. Larry said so, and he knew. She wouldn't need them again.

The Man Who Told the Truth

She thought: This is how a prisoner feels, seeing the doors swing open at last, knowing the sunlight outside is free for him to walk in. This *is* freedom. She picked up the wastebasket, thinking she would empty the pills into the fireplace. But that would imply she was afraid to have them around. She wasn't. Instead, she'd take a bath and put on her prettiest dress. Maybe she'd even wash her hair and try it a new way. The minute Bill stepped into the house he must be made to realize this was a special and wonderful evening.

Bill Thorndyke placed a paper on top of the pile that lay on his desk and then checked to be sure they were all there. The bank was very quiet. Except for himself and Shelley Carew, the building was empty.

He wished he didn't have to put this extra bit of business off on her. She was so young to be saddled with all this. He could never get over the feeling that her life was wasted here. What good was the Carew money if it gave her nothing but trouble and work?

A fine one he was to talk of wasted lives! Certainly the Thorndyke money—less than the Carew holdings, but still no small sum—had not brought happiness to him or to Ursula. On the contrary, there were times when he felt it stood in the way. It might even account for Ursula's invalidism. She used it as an escape from a situation with which she had never been able to cope, brought up as she had been in a family where there was never any money at all.

He touched the papers once more, his hand trembling a little. An old man's gesture of resignation and defeat, he thought wearily.

He could no longer delay showing these papers to Shelley. They were the records of her father's various philanthropies and now, in December, it was necessary to give attention to such things, with the year ending and income-tax reports soon due. Before they could be turned over to the tax accountant, Shelley must pass on them; her signature would be necessary if the gifts were to continue another year.

He stood up and took one more look at her. How beautiful she was! Those Oriental-looking eyes, that rich olive skin, the smooth dark hair, the rounded curves of arms and ankles, the proud way she carried her head, even the exotic perfume she wore—all these combined to make even the soberest-minded male pause and consider her. And Bill Thorndyke discovered, in an emotion somewhere between amazement and satisfaction, that he himself was not sober-minded by nature. As he prepared to go to Shelley's office, he felt himself blushing like a boy. Good Lord—he might have been twenty once more and setting out on a spring day to meet a girl. He wasn't at all his own staid forty-one, preparing only to take some papers across to a young girl working at her desk.

The Man Who Told the Truth

He wondered, as he so often did these days, what had happened between Shelley and Larry Beckwith. Jim Carew had seemed very sure they would marry—or else why had he taken the steps that he had? Surely the man had explained all these to Larry ahead of time. And yet Bill Thorndyke could not get out of his mind two things; the cagey way Larry had acted when the committee asked him to take over Dr. Grayson's practice, and the attitude he had displayed upon seeing the papers concerning the practice. But again, Larry could not have helped knowing about these conditions all along. He had got all the concessions he wanted, hadn't he? So it must have been only a coincidence that the engagement was broken at the same time Larry agreed to come back to Benson to practice.

Anyway, so far as anyone knew now—even Miss Stacie had no additional information to offer—the two young people never saw each other. Of course Shelley was in Dallas a great deal, but even so, in a town the size of Benson, people were bound to run into each other unless they took pains to avoid it.

Bill walked across the lobby now and went to the open door of Shelley's office. She wore a pale green dress, softly tailored and vastly becoming. At his entrance she looked up to smile at him, and, as always, he thought she had one of the loveliest smiles he had ever seen. It lighted up a face that could seem slightly arrogant in repose, and gave it warmth and humor.

"Come in," she said. And then she made a face. "Ugh —more papers! I thought I was through for the day."

"These shouldn't give you much difficulty. But I thought since the year is about finished you'd better look at them. They are the records of your father's charities. You remember, I told you."

"I said we'd go along with them, whatever they are."

"I know. But the way they're set up, your father looked them over at the end of each year, and then if he wanted to continue, he signed a new order. He always did continue them, I may as well tell you, but nonetheless he went through the routine of signing."

"All right, let's get at them."

So they began to go over them together, considering each charity separately. The contribution that formed the major part of Miss Stacie's salary, together with the stipulation that the building in which the library was housed would be rent-free; the money lent to the Methodist Church, which bore a ridiculously low rate of interest; the provisions governing the small shoe factory Jim Carew had been instrumental in bringing to Benson because the town needed more employment opportunities—the list was long and varied. Shelley fastened her attention on each one, considering it a moment and then signing the authorization to continue it. Finally there was only one paper remaining.

"I left this until last," Bill told her, "because it's a little more complicated than the others."

He saw her begin to read it, and almost immediately a puzzled frown came over her face. Her eyes raced down the first page; she turned it to read the next. Then she went back, rereading carefully, as if she did not believe what she had first seen. The color drained from her face; suddenly she covered her face in her hands and began to cry.

"Shelley," he said anxiously, reaching out to touch her shoulder awkwardly, "is—is something wrong? I mean, are you ill?"

She lifted her head to stare at him, disbelief darkening her eyes.

"You mean, from the first—all along—the provisions for the hospital have been like this?"

"You didn't know?"

"No," she said. "I didn't know. Tell me."

So he tried to explain her father's original provisions, the way they had been set aside, the plan in use now.

"So that was it," she said softly. "I might have known."

She stood up quickly, extending her hands in a helpless gesture as she did so. Her face was twisted with pain, making her look frightened and vulnerable. Bill Thorndyke reached out instinctively to put his arm around her. She dropped her head on his shoulder and his arm tightened. He could feel the tenseness of her body.

He said, "Shelley, my dear," softly and comfortingly, even though his senses were singing at her touch. "Shelley . . ." he repeated.

As suddenly as she had turned to him, she broke away. Scarcely seeming aware of him at all, she took her coat from the hanger, picked up her bag and gloves and hurried out the door. Bill Thorndyke stood uncertainly, watching her leave the bank, seeing her slim, tense body silhouetted against the winter sky. Then he picked up the papers and placed them all in a drawer. This done, he too left the building.

He had some notion of following Shelley—who had left in her car, driving much too fast, he noted—but then discarded the idea. He had his own problems to consider, and they were all the more disturbing because they had been thrust upon him in such an unexpected manner.

That brief touch had held a kind of magic, bringing back memories of warmth and love and happiness, qualities he had thought long since dead in himself. There had been a time when Ursula had meant these things to him; they had meant this to each other.

But they had gone on so long in their present relationship that by now it seemed hard to remember they had once had another kind of life. He supposed for the most part it was his fault. If he tried, could he break through the barriers between them? How would he go about it?

The Man Who Told the Truth

Ursula, I'm sorry. . . .

Sorry for what? That the habit of being polite strangers was so fixed between them now that breaking it would be harder than maintaining it?

Ursula, let's back off and make a fresh start. . . .

Start what? There had never been a pattern of rightness for them to recapture. Except for those few months in Florida their life together had always been shadowed by some force outside themselves—her accident, the well-meant domination of his parents, her invalidism, even her dislike for the house in which they lived. Gradually over the years he had come to accept these things as inevitable, living in a kind of numbed acceptance, finding as his one antidote the demands the bank made upon him. Now he wondered if all these things were as inevitable as they had always seemed.

But even as he faced up to his own responsibility in the matter, he knew that without Ursula's help he could do little or nothing to correct the situation. And perhaps he had waited too long to expect Ursula to help.

In his deep concentration he had passed his own house. He turned back, climbed the steps, and unlocked the front door. Ursula would probably be in her room, he thought, although in the weeks since Paul Mitchell had got her interested in knitting she was sometimes in the den. But this evening he found her in the living room. There was a fire in the grate and she was dressed as if for a party. Perhaps Mitchell had phoned he was coming for dinner, Bill thought. It wouldn't surprise him a bit.

Ursula came running toward him, her cheeks flushed, her eyes bright.

"Ursula," he began, bracing himself. He must talk to her, but she showed every intention of taking over the conversation herself. "Ursula!" he repeated in some alarm, thinking maybe she had taken an overdose of medicine.

"Oh, Bill!" she cried, throwing her arms around his neck, a gesture as unexpected as her excited manner. "Darling, the most wonderful thing has happened."

He stood quietly, making no motion either to draw away or to return her embrace, mesmerized by the joy and delight in her face.

"Bill," she went on, "I've been to see Dr. Beckwith. I was feeling simply awful this morning and I got scared and went to him. And he says—oh, I can't believe it, but he says there's no doubt about it!" She stopped, carried away by her own wonder at what Larry Beckwith had told her. "He says I'm going to have a baby!"

Bill stood, stunned by the impact of her words, incapable of either believing or disbelieving.

"Bill—did you hear me? I said we're going to have a baby!"

He thought: I ought to be able to think of something to say instead of standing here stupid and frozen. I should be able to rise up to meet this happiness of hers. But all he could think of was that perhaps it was something she had dreamed up as she lay drugged with her pills.

He cleared his throat. "Are you sure?" he found himself asking awkwardly.

"Oh, yes—very sure. And I'm all right. I'm fine. You needn't be worried a bit. Dr. Larry says I'll come through with no trouble." She looked at him anxiously. "You mustn't be worried, honey," she went on softly. "I'll be all right. Lots of women my age have babies."

At her words, the numbness and the shock left him. He mustn't worry, she said—wanting first of all to think of him. A realization of what she had told him began to take over. They were going to have a child, like all the other couples they knew, like most of the married people all over the world—the ones who made up the world now and the ones going back to the dimmest beginnings of history, and those who would come after them. Our children and our children's children, he thought. A whole new generation was having its beginning with them, a continuity as endless as time itself.

There was a thundering in his heart, and above it he heard himself saying, "Ursula, dear . . ." And as he spoke, he held her very tight.

Martha Donnell was wearing her comfortable old terry-cloth robe, long since faded into muted off-color streaks.

The pockets were stuffed with tissues and her eyes and nose were red. She had a cold.

She wasn't feverish, but even so, since this was Friday, she had decided to stay at home from school. It wasn't right to go spreading germs among the children, and in her opinion any teacher who felt virtuous for dragging herself to school under such circumstances was crazy.

Surprisingly, considering how she felt, the day had been rather pleasant. She hadn't even dressed. Just before time for supper she had taken a bath and got into her nightgown and oldest robe, which was by far the most comfortable thing she had. She had heated up some soup for herself and sent Clark across to Mrs. Higdon's for his evening meal. Then she settled down on the divan, an afghan over her, a book in her hand, a glass of water and a bottle of aspirin beside her—sheepishly admitting to herself that she was rather enjoying this cold. She heard Clark come in and when he said he was going to watch television she dozed and felt much at peace.

She was in that pleasant state, halfway between sleeping and waking, when she heard the front door open. She gave no thought to it. Clark had probably gone outside for something and was coming back in again.

"Clark?" she called, out of sheer habit.

There was no answer, so she got up to see who it was. She was standing beside the couch when Paul Mitchell walked into the room.

He came straight to where she stood. Her first instinct was to crawl back under the afghan and cover up even her head.

"Clark said you were ill," he began, without preliminaries. "I mean—you weren't at supper, and he said you were ill."

"It's just a cold," she told him, and wondered why he looked at her so oddly. "It's nothing," she said. "Just sniffles. They're going the rounds now."

He still didn't look at ease. What *had* Clark told him? Children sometimes exaggerated things for drama's sake.

"I looked across the table and saw that you weren't there, Martha," he said slowly, as if he had just gone through some harrowing experience. "You weren't there with Clark, and suddenly I had to come."

As simply and naturally as if he acted like this every time he came, he put his arms around her.

"Darling Martha," he said, "I couldn't stand it—for you to be ill, and here alone."

Then he kissed her.

Martha had been kissed before, of course—any number of times. But in these last years it had been mostly by aging widowers who needed someone to look after their families and reasoned that no woman could be better at this than a teacher. Sometimes they would state their proposal just that frankly, finishing it off with, "How about it, Martha?" Then, often without waiting for an answer (if they hadn't all been so sure she'd take them without even hesitating, she might have given one or two of them serious consideration), they would grab her and land an awkward kiss somewhere in the vicinity of her mouth. Their ardor always struck her as more ridiculous than romantic.

Still, she had felt the need for refusing them without hurting their pride. At first she had had Mama and Papa, and then later Papa alone, as an excuse. Of course she could not leave them. And so she had got rid of her half-hearted suitors with no hurt feelings on anyone's part, rejecting them as husbands while keeping them as friends.

But this was different. She relaxed against Paul Mitchell, feeling a great shyness taking possession of her and at the same time a surging sweetness. She would not push this man away. She wanted to be where she was, in his arms. It didn't even seem to matter that she looked dreadful and had a red nose.

She lifted her arms and linked them around his neck. He kissed her again, and this time she returned his kiss.

Then just as suddenly as he had taken her in his arms he pushed her away. There was a strange, surprised look in his eyes. Too stunned to speak or even to act intelligently, she stood still, her arms still around his neck.

He reached up and drew her arms down to her sides.

Without a word he turned and walked out of the room.

She took a couple of quick steps toward the door, thinking to call after him. But instead she walked to the front door as circumspectly as she could bring herself to do and peered out through the glass.

Paul stood on the sidewalk, clearly visible under the street light. Even after his strange behavior he still had the power to make her yearn for him, looking lonely and dejected under the winter sky.

As she looked, Shelley Carew's car rocketed past the house. She must be doing ninety, Martha thought. Crazy! What was the girl trying to do?

The car made an abrupt turn at the corner with a tortured screech of tires and headed south. Why should Shelley choose that road? It was a narrow, rutted country lane that came to a dead end a couple of miles out of town, just beyond a rickety wooden bridge.

She saw Paul turn to watch the car as it careened out of sight. Then after a moment's hesitation he walked away in the direction the car had gone. When he was out of sight she went back to the couch and threw herself down on it. She didn't often cry, but she cried now.

- 8 -

SHELLEY CAREW RACED ALONG THE NARROW ROAD, TAKING A strange, savage pleasure in pushing her car faster than she knew was safe. She had not chosen this road deliberately, having turned more from instinct than from actual motive, but now that she was on it she was glad. She had it to herself, which was what she wanted—to be alone, her mind free to contemplate the stunning knowledge that had come to her only a short time ago.

So *that* was why Larry had acted as he did! Now she understood his rage; now she knew why he assumed she had been a party to the whole humiliating business. It was clear at last—terribly, inescapably clear. No wonder his anger had moved him to lash out at her.

She should have known, she thought now. Larry was not a man to fly into rages without reason. And her own stunned silence must have seemed to him an admission of her part in the matter.

Why hadn't her father told her? Now, as she looked back, she thought that perhaps he had tried to. But she had not wanted to listen, thinking she knew all too well why Larry had turned against her, finding the assumption only too painful to dwell upon. And so she and her father had dropped the subject and never reopened it, both of them side-stepping the issue of the broken engagement—as if by ignoring the fact they would make it cease to exist.

Even now she was honest enough to admit part of the reason for Larry's defection. He had finally found the strength to reject her. She had been the aggressor in their relationship always, and what she had taken for love was merely acceptance—a good and decent young man's facing up to the inevitable. But this gesture on her father's part had seemed nothing more than outright purchase to him, as if he were a beribboned gift under Shelley's Christmas tree.

Even this evening, her first impulse after leaving the bank was to run down the street to the Beckwith house, throw open the door, and cry out, "Larry, I didn't know! Honestly, I didn't! Not until this afternoon . . ."

But she had caught herself in time and gone home. Run after Larry again? No. Someday she would tell him, but with dignity and self-control, giving him no occasion to think it meant more to her than any other business deal her father had been involved in and of which she had only recently been informed.

Once she was at home, though, she had not been able to bear the emptiness of the house. She had snatched a coat from the closet, picked up her bag and gone to her car. In a moment she was off, roaring through the evening darkness. Now she didn't know how long she had been driving, any more than she knew why she had chosen this road.

And what a road it was! Even as she had the thought, the car hit a spot so rough that the door, which she must have failed to close properly, swung open. Not bothering to slow down, she reached across the seat to shut it.

The car swerved. There was a skidding sensation so swift it took her breath. She felt herself being caught up and flipped, like a rock sent from a slingshot. There was a second of intense pain as she was dragged across the seat and then flung through the air. When she hit the ground there was no feeling at all except a dreadful numbness.

She pushed it back, fighting to stay conscious. She was lying in a shallow ditch at the side of the road. The sight of the car, hanging precariously half over the ditch and half in the road, was frightening enough to clear her head. She must get into the car and set it straight on the road. Tilted as it was, it could fall over on her.

She tried to get up. She couldn't move. She tried again. Nothing happened, except that she felt a blinding pain. Then, mercifully, she was swallowed up in blackness.

The Man Who Told the Truth

She had no way of knowing how long it was before she came back to consciousness. Her first thought was: I've got to get back into the car. It still stood tilted dangerously over where she lay. She tried tentatively to drag herself upright, only to find she was no more able to move now than she had been before. Finally she lay still, knowing there was nothing she could do for herself.

Her one hope lay in having someone drive by and find her —but this, she knew, might take hours. This was a seldom-used road. No one knew she had taken it, and there was no one at home to send out a search party if she failed to return at a reasonable hour. She faced the possibility that she might have to lie here all night before anyone discovered her.

Fortunately—and she forced herself to dwell on this—the night was not very cold. Also, either because she had inadvertently flipped the ignition key as she hurtled from behind the wheel, or because fate was looking after her, the car engine was not running. And although the front wheels were over the edge of the ditch where she lay, the car seemed firmly enough anchored on the road and showed no indication of being ready to topple over upon her. In fact, she thought, the very oddness of its position would encourage investigation by anyone who passed by. . . .

Lying there—and she did not know whether she was half unconscious or only half asleep—was very pleasant. She seemed to be running down the street, the cold wind stinging her cheeks, trying to overtake Larry Beckwith. "Larry," she called, "Larry!"

"No," she heard a voice saying. "No—it's me—Paul Mitchell. You're hurt."

"I can't move," she told him, and felt a surge of impatience. How stupid could a man be? He was just standing there looking at her and at the car hanging crazily above her.

"You go for help!" she said, her anger at his attitude almost overcoming her pain. "Take my car."

"I—I can't drive," he told her stupidly.

"Then walk," she said. "But go—please!"

She drifted into unconsciousness again, only to be brought back by the sound of her car backing away from the ditch, turning, heading toward town.

Strange thoughts danced through her mind, advancing, retreating, like children doing a ballet. Paul Mitchell had driven her car away. No, it couldn't be Mitchell—he had said he couldn't drive. Whoever it was had put a blanket over her before leaving. That was more like Larry—except that Larry wouldn't have left her. . . . Oh, yes, he had left her once. . . . But sometimes he waited.

She was a child again, running down the street, her pigtails flying out behind her. Larry was a block away. Unless he waited, she could never overtake him. For some reason it seemed very important, more so than it ever had before.

"Larry!" she called desperately. "Larry, wait a minute. I'm coming!"

Larry Beckwith sat in his office doing nothing at all. Occasionally he came back in the evenings, wanting a look at the place when it was not running over with patients. Not that he disliked patients—on the contrary, he liked them very much indeed. But they gave him little chance to think his own thoughts, to look around the office and know that even if it was not actually his as yet, it was in the process of becoming so.

True, it was small, but more than adequate for a town the size of Benson. The waiting room and inner office had been enough in themselves for Dr. Grayson, but now there was also an X-ray room, a treatment room, and another small room where he could keep a patient a few hours or even overnight if the need arose. All these were so new they still smelled faintly of paint.

As he sat there, he recalled the day the committee from Benson had come to Austin, where he was interning, to offer him this office. He was within a few months of finishing his internship and he was feeling a sense of power and pride. The date of his marriage was so close—contingent only on his finding a good location in which to practice.

He was already considering several possibilities—chances to go in with established doctors. His choice was somewhat limited—since, by and large, people these days preferred doctors who had specialized. Still, general practitioners were coming back into their own, and if he joined forces with an established group, he could get good training and perhaps specialize later. The important thing now was that he could find a place and support a wife—maybe not in the fashion to which she had been accustomed, but after his own fashion. Which, he thought with a grin, would be pretty darned good if Shelley shared it.

While he was considering these pleasant prospects the committee from Benson had come to see him.

It was headed by Bill Thorndyke. Jim Carew was not with them—which was strange, Larry thought, for Carew usually got his finger into every pie that was baked in Benson. He was, however, inordinately glad for the omission. Old Man Carew's presence would have suggested only one thing—he was buying a doctor-husband for his daughter.

The committee seemed oddly ill at ease—probably, Larry thought, because they were unaccustomed to handling any civic enterprise without Jim Carew's benign guidance. Finally, after some hemming and hawing they did manage to make known their proposition. In essence, it was simple. Would Larry, when he finished his internship, come to Benson to practice? Since Dr. Grayson's death the town had been without a doctor. They were prepared to buy Dr. Grayson's building from his heirs and in addition add such rooms as Larry—Dr. Beckwith—might think advisable. They were also prepared to guarantee a salary. They named it and then asked what his reaction was.

His impulse was to shout, Yes, thanks a lot! He wanted to run to the phone and tell the good news to Shelley. Things were all worked out, they could marry and he could support her himself.

But he restrained himself, his natural doctor's caution taking over. He was a physician, examining all the symptoms before making a diagnosis. How would it be financed?

The members of the committee hesitated, looking at one another.

"You have a plan?" Larry asked.

Oh, yes, indeed, they had a plan. Everything was all worked out. They outlined it while he listened, and it sounded good enough. Sensible and well thought out. Larry listened and made up his mind.

"I'll take it," he said, keeping his voice level only by a conscious effort. "Provided there is a clause in the contract stipulating that I can buy the whole outfit from you as soon as I am able."

They looked at one another doubtfully, evidently not prepared for this turn of events. Finally Bill Thorndyke, who was chairman, cleared his throat and said, "Sure. Yes, indeed. It can undoubtedly be arranged."

"I'd like it written into the contract," Larry said.

Again there was the faint hesitation.

"I'm sure that can be arranged," Bill Thorndyke said again. "Although, of course, we hadn't—well, anticipated doing this. But—yes, I'm sure it can be worked out. When you come to Benson to look things over, just drop by the bank and I'll have the papers ready."

"Just one more thing," Larry told them. "No salary guarantee. I'll manage on what I make in fees."

"Well, if that's your wish——"

"It is." As indeed it was. He'd buy the clinic, small though it might be, with his own money, not with handouts from the town.

Once the committee was gone, he raced to the phone to call Shelley long-distance. He could afford it now.

"Shelley," he cried joyously across the miles. "The most wonderful news . . ."

"Silly," she said. "I already know. Everyone up here is flipping at the idea of having you as our doctor." She paused a moment. "I think I'll come down there so we can celebrate."

"You stay right where you are," he told her. At last he had the right to lay down conditions to her. "I'm coming up there."

"When?"

"Next month. I'll be through with the internship then."

"And we can be married?"

"You're a pushy female! But, yes, we can be married—as soon as I collect my first fees."

"Yes, master," he heard the faint edge of a giggle in her voice. "Just make it soon, will you?"

By the time he arrived in Benson, the new addition to Dr. Grayson's office was well on the way to being finished. Larry walked around the building, pleased at the progress. This taken care of, he cut across to the bank. He'd have a look at the contract to be sure all the details were settled to his liking, and then he'd sign. After that, he'd go to Shelley. "Here I am, honey," he'd tell her. "A full-fledged doctor, ready to take over a practice and support a wife. Name the day."

At the bank, Bill Thorndyke seemed glad to see him. "Good to have you back, Larry," he said.

"Good to be here. I thought I'd have a look at those papers now."

"Sure, sure . . ."

Larry wondered if he only imagined the trace of hesitation in Bill's voice as he led the way to his office, where Bill spread out the papers on his desk. It was then that Larry found out the truth.

Actually, there *was* no committee except in name. The whole arrangement had been sparked by Jim Carew. It was he who had bought the office from the Grayson heirs, who had underwritten the additions to the original building, who was the source of the salary guarantee. He had used the committee as cover for his scheme.

Larry was too stupefied to speak.

"Don't you understand the details?" Bill Thorndyke finally asked. "It's all spelled out, right here in these papers."

"Yes," Larry said, "I understand."

He understood, all right. Old Man Carew was buying him, just as he had bought the library and the factory and all the other things he had furnished the town. If he bought them, why not a doctor too, all equipped with a clinic and a guaranteed salary? But he wasn't doing this for the town. This was for Shelley.

Want him, Baby? I'll get him for you. . . .

Shelley knew about this; of course she did. She had known before he did. Hadn't she told him so when he called her? She and her father and the whole town were rejoicing over the purchase even before he himself had agreed to it. They were certain he would come, certain that the Carew money would buy this item for Benson just as it had bought so many others. Just as it had gratified every whim of Shelley's.

"I told Mr. Carew about your wish to buy the practice eventually, and he said that was all right if it's what you want. Although it wasn't really necessary. He had planned to give it as a wedding gift," Bill explained.

Shaking with anger and humiliation, Larry got to his feet. It was on the tip of his tongue to say they could have their damned practice—he'd have no part of it. A doctor was not for sale. Old Hippocrates himself had been quite explicit on this matter. Medicine was not a trade or a commodity; a doctor belonged to an ancient and honorable profession, and he set his own conditions and made his own decisions. He was *not* a wedding gift for a bride who had everything.

And then another thought came to him. He would take the job, but on his own conditions.

"Hand me that paper," he said levelly.

He took it and read it carefully, noting that it gave him the right to buy the place as soon as he was able to. He read it twice, just to be sure there was no hidden clause, no fine print.

Then he fixed his name to it and handed it to Bill Thorndyke.

"Here," he said. "Just show this to Mr. Carew when he comes into the bank."

He turned and walked out, across the square and down the streets to the Carew house. There he went inside and broke his engagement to Shelley. He did it cruelly—he knew that now—for in his own hurt and humiliation he was incapable of kindness. He did it without explanation, for she knew as well as he did what was behind his action. He did it with such conviction and finality that she had to accept his decision.

Then he left the house without looking back.

The following week the Carews had left on their world cruise and Larry Beckwith had moved into his new office.

Those were the memories that came back to Larry now as he sat in his office. He shifted his weight in the chair—Dr. Grayson's chair—and thought how often the old doctor must have sat here, thinking over problems of life and death. Other people's life and death. Did a doctor ever have time to think of his own worries? Larry wondered. Was there always something else in the way? Perhaps he didn't even have a *right* to think of himself.

But that was crazy. A doctor was human like anybody else, with the same needs and responses and frailties and strengths. There was no reason for him to think he ought to be so dedicated as always to push his own interests aside. If he did that, he would be an insufferable prig.

In any case, he told himself, he'd better go home and get some rest. He went to the door of the office, flicked off the light and went out.

Just as he stepped outside a car drove up and stopped. He caught his breath when he saw the car was Shelley's. He had to look twice, though, before he could believe it was Paul Mitchell who got out. Mitchell had said he didn't drive.

"Larry," Paul Mitchell began abruptly, "there's been an accident . . ."

"Shelley!" Larry said, feeling the name come out stiff and

strange. "Is she—"

"No, she's alive. I thought I'd better not move her, so I covered her with a blanket and left her there."

"That's good," Larry told him, his doctor's mind instantly alert. "Go get Ben Langley's delivery truck, so she can lie flat. I'll get my bag and a stretcher."

"All right," Mitchell said and started off. Then he turned to say over his shoulder, "Bring whatever you think is necessary, but leave your blasted pride at home. She's calling your name—keeps saying something about not knowing until today . . ."

He hurried off, heading for Langley's.

Afterward, Larry remembered the way Paul Mitchell seemed to be everywhere he was needed—driving Langley's pickup to the scene of the accident, helping to lift Shelley onto the stretcher and make her comfortable in the back of the truck, driving the truck back to town. At the time, however, Larry was conscious only of Shelley. He seemed to live a thousand lifetimes before they reached her, lying there in the roadside ditch.

"I'm here, darling," he told her. "Everything is going to be all right."

She looked up at him and whispered so softly he had to bend low to catch her words. "You did wait," she said.

"I'll always wait, my dearest," he told her. "Always, after this, I'll be right there waiting for you."

Ben Langley was more than a little disgusted. For all the business he was doing he might as well close the store. Nobody in town wanted to do anything except talk about Shelley Carew's accident. Men gathered in knots on the street; women held up the lines to discuss it over the phone. Everybody was saying much the same thing—wasn't it God's own miracle she had come out of it as well as she had, with only a few broken bones? Dr. Beckwith said it himself.

The women were adding their own footnotes to the story. Already they had noticed, with twitterings of delight, that Larry Beckwith's concern went beyond mere professional interest. By now, Ben thought, the women had planned the wedding, settled the young couple and likely as not named the first two children. Women!

Ben himself was more concerned about another matter. It was nine thirty in the morning and Paul Mitchell had not yet come to work. At least a dozen people had dropped by, making no pretense of wanting to buy anything, merely to see Paul and congratulate him for getting help to Shelley in time. If she had lain there on that lonely road all night, there was no telling what might have happened.

Ben stood it as long as he could. Then he went to the phone and called Mrs. Higdon's.

"Hello, Daisy," he said when Mrs. Higdon answered. "I want to talk to Paul Mitchell."

"Isn't he at the store?" Daisy asked.

"No. Call him, will you?"

She left, and after what seemed a long time she was back. "He's gone," she said, sounding as if she didn't believe it herself.

"What do you mean—gone?" Ben yelled into the phone.

"I mean—he's not in his room," Daisy said.

"Didn't he come in last night?"

"Yes."

Usually Daisy was as levelheaded as they came, Ben thought, but now she was so excited he had a hard time getting the story out of her. Eventually, though, he managed to piece together what she was telling him.

Paul Mitchell had come in late last night. Daisy heard him moving around in his room for a while and then she dropped off to sleep. He didn't come down for breakfast this morning but she thought nothing of it, for he sometimes slipped out early without eating. When she had gone to his room just now he wasn't there. The bed hadn't been slept in. There was an envelope on the table containing his room-and-board money, and that was it. Not a word of explanation.

Ben hung up the receiver and stood there thinking for a long time. Then he started toward the men's department with the intention of checking the cash register. After the first impulsive step, he stopped. He would not do it. He'd stake his life on a bet that everything was in order there. If

Paul Mitchell wanted to leave town without accounting to anyone, it was his right. Tomorrow or the next day there would be a letter from Mitchell himself.

The next day did bring a bit of news, but not from Mitchell. The bus driver said yes, a man had boarded the early-morning bus. Might have been Mitchell; the description fitted him all right. The driver distinctly remembered the scar. When pressed for further details, he said that the man had got off at Oklahoma City.

"Likely had business there," Ben retorted gruffly when he heard the news. "We'll hear all about it in a few days."

They did hear in a few days, but not quite in the way Ben had in mind.

The story appeared on the front page of a Dallas paper. More than a year ago a grade-school principal in Tennessee, driving a school bus for the regular driver who was ill, had skidded off a curve on a hilly road and plunged into the river below. Since it was almost the end of the line, only six children were on the bus. The young principal had acted the hero's part, diving into the icy water to rescue the children trapped in the bus. He had brought up four of them, injured but alive. Two were dead before he could bring them to the surface.

The driver himself had been so gravely injured that he was hospitalized pending an inquiry into the accident. Then one night he disappeared from the hospital without leaving a clue as to where he had gone. Now, without warning, the young principal had returned to Tennessee to the scene of the accident. There followed a few more details about the man. He had been an excellent teacher, a civic-minded, highly respected citizen. He was a widower, his wife having been dead three years. There were no children.

Ben Langley read the story through carefully. He did not need the accompanying picture to identify the man about whom it was written. Paul Mitchell, of course.

His phone rang shrilly. He had a good mind not to answer —a dozen people in Benson took the Dallas paper.

- 9 -

MISS STACIE SNIFFED THE APRIL AIR, FEELING A RICH AND SEN-
suous delight. April was a wonderful month—warm and
sunny, with blue skies and the shrubs and trees turning
green. This was good weather for Bess Dawson's arthritis.

But, fine as the weather was, it did not give her the solid
satisfaction that the new sign offered. It was a big, bold one,
newly installed and easy to read from a distance. It said,
"Benson Public Library."

Miss Stacie regarded it now, proudly. She supposed she
was a fool, but having the sign made her feel better. It was
as if by installing it she had put up a memorial to Paul Mitchell, who had stayed five months in this town and put his
mark for good on it. It was strange, in a way, that nobody in
Benson had blamed him very much for what had happened
in Tennessee, or even for his masquerading—if that was
what you could call it—here. There were bound to be reasons for what he did; a man had a right to conceal his past

if he wanted to. Everyone was more inclined to remember, and with reason, the good things Paul Mitchell had done for so many of them.

For instance, he had probably saved Shelley's life. Now she was as well as anyone, married to Larry Beckwith and both of them as happy as could be. And it was common knowledge that Ursula Thorndyke's recovery was partly due to Mitchell, who had got her interested in knitting and helped her get over being frightened of having people come to the house. Now the Thorndykes were in Florida on what Bill called a second honeymoon, and in a few months their baby would be born.

Ben Langley's store was a different place these days, and that was Paul Mitchell's influence too. It really paid to shop there now, Miss Stacie thought. In the old days, Ben would hold his stock forever, but now he had frequent specials, and so his merchandise was always fresh and up to date.

Perhaps Martha Donnell had been helped as much as anyone by Paul Mitchell's stay in Benson. She had needed a man to help out with Clark, and Mitchell had been good about giving her a hand. Clark played baseball with the other boys now, and when they chose their teams, Clark was often picked first—mainly because Paul Mitchell had taught him how to pitch.

Martha herself was looking thin, Miss Stacie thought— thin and nervous and edgy. Most people probably thought she was merely working too hard. Miss Stacie, however, had other ideas about what was wrong, and her heart ached for the girl.

Martha would get over it in time—girls had always done so and would continue to, the world and human nature being what they were. Miss Stacie herself had experience along those lines. Her mind flicked back to a spring when she was young, when just seeing Jim Carew at a distance had lent a glory to her day, when she had every reason to believe he had felt the same way about her.

Then one day he had come back from Dallas unexpectedly (as much a surprise to him as to the town, some people said) with a brand-new wife. And what a life Nellie Carew had led him, with her vagueness and her ill health! But she made up for this by giving him Shelley.

And so Stacie had found meaning in life in her library. Oh, no one could know better than she both the nature and depth of Martha's hurt and the fact that she would manage. For Martha Donnell had her salvation ready at hand; she had Clark.

Yes, Martha would manage. But Miss Stacie wished devoutly that it didn't have to be that way.

"There's a man here to see you, Dr. Beckwith," Miss Williams said, putting her head in at the door. Her cap was sitting at an angle, her eyes round with wonder.

Larry's first reaction was one of annoyance. He had hoped
to get off early this afternoon. He had half promised Shelley,
though warning her that she mustn't expect it. And she had
said—quite meekly for her (although he knew that mocking
mischief was just below the surface)—that she didn't mind
so long as she was sure he would be along eventually. And
she said she didn't know why she had married him in the
first place—might as well have a traveling man for a husband. Then she had kissed him good-by and he went off to
the office, reflecting briefly that it was hard to believe any
one man could be this happy.

"Show him in," Larry said now to Miss Williams.

The nurse stepped aside, and Paul Mitchell walked into
the office.

Larry got abruptly to his feet. He said, "Well, I'll be—"
And then, more formally, "Well, hello!"

Mitchell stood hesitantly in front of the desk. Even
through his own astonishment, Larry realized there was
something different about the man. He was embarrassed,
naturally enough, for he had disappeared from town three
months ago with no explanation. Now, just as abruptly, he
was back.

And yet in spite of his obvious unease, he seemed more
sure of himself than he had before. The vagueness was gone,

147

Larry saw, and the remoteness.

"Sit down," Larry said. He sat down himself, all thoughts of going home having left him.

Paul Mitchell took a chair and looked across the desk at him. "You know?" he asked.

"Yes, we read the papers. We know the general details."

Mitchell hesitated, seeming to grope for words.

"See here," Larry said, feeling awkward. After all, this man had come back after what must have been a rough experience and he shouldn't feel he had to rehash it for anybody's benefit. "Look, Paul—you don't have to tell us any more than you want. If you'd rather not, that is . . ."

"I'd rather, if you don't mind. I want to tell you a few things and then ask some questions. You have time?"

"All the time in the world," Larry assured him.

"First, you must believe I wasn't playing a trick on you. I had forgotten. There was a piece of bone pressing in on my brain. I've had an operation. I'm all right now—there's nothing at all wrong any more."

"As far as we were concerned," Larry interrupted, "we never did think there was anything wrong with you."

Paul Mitchell smiled. "Now," he continued, "I want to know: Did I do anything—well, out of the way in the months I was here? Or say anything?"

"Well," Larry began vaguely. His impulse was to make a joke out of the matter, but after looking at Mitchell's earnest face he knew he must be serious. "No, there was nothing out of the way."

"I remember some things I said—times when I was almost rude in my frankness. Am I right?"

"Oh, that—well, you did tell us some plain truths about ourselves now and then. But it was good for us. Mostly we've been the better for it."

"Strange," Mitchell mused, "because it seems part of my trouble stemmed from the fact that I wouldn't face up to my own difficulty. They said it was from that as much as from the blow on the head. I wouldn't, or couldn't, admit I was—" he hesitated, looked quickly away and swallowed a couple of times—"responsible for the death of those children."

"But you weren't responsible," Larry reminded him. "The papers said that the mechanic failed to check the bus properly."

"I should have double-checked his work."

"But you didn't," Larry said softly.

"I didn't, and that's a fact I must learn to live with."

"We all have them," Larry said.

" '. . . nor all your tears wash out a word of it,' " Paul Mitchell quoted wryly.

"Old Omar the tentmaker," Larry said with a grin. "I haven't thought of him since I was a college freshman."

"I've thought of him a great deal in the past few months," Mitchell said. And then, changing the subject abruptly, he

149

continued: "Now, is this what happened?"

He went on to sketch his stay in the town, and occasionally Larry would say, "Yes, that's right," or nod briefly. Strange how much Mitchell seemed to remember—his work at Langley's, staying at Daisy Higdon's, playing chess at Bill Thorndyke's. Larry listened, making no attempt to prompt him. Let the story come out as it would.

"I seem to remember that I liked this town. It resembled the one I had left in Kansas, but for some reason I can't remember that town very well at all. I went back there to check. They tell me I worked in a store, and was quiet and gave no one any trouble. Then one day I left abruptly, and all I know beyond that is that I showed up here one morning."

"That's nothing against you," Larry said.

"I seem to remember—or at least, I think I do—that I made a sort of place for myself here. Right?"

"Right."

"There must have been times when I was close to remembering all that had happened. But I'd deliberately, if unconsciously, shut out the thought just as it was about to come clear to me. Maybe those were the times when I was so blunt —made you people face up to yourselves, as you so tactfully phrase it."

"Could be. I sometimes think that the people who go around working out other people's problems are the ones who refuse to face their own," Larry said.

"And then that night I came upon the wreck—Shelley Carew's wreck—"

"She's Shelley Beckwith now," Larry told him.

"She is? Well, congratulations! At any rate, when I came upon the wreck, all of a sudden it hit me: the past, the present, everything. I knew what I had done back in Tennessee. I knew where I was. Oh, there were gaps; there still are. But mostly, I knew. Do you believe me?"

"Of course. The mind can play strange tricks on us—all the stranger when we ourselves will it to."

"My first reaction was that I must go back to Tennessee and face things. And that's what I did," Mitchell said. "I faced it. And now I'm here to face anything else I may need to face."

"There is nothing," Larry assured him. "You did only good things in this town."

Mitchell hadn't mentioned Martha Donnell, Larry thought. Was this something he didn't want to recall?

Mitchell stood up. He hesitated, a flush coming over his face. "I seem to remember there was a woman I was fond of," he said quietly. "A teacher."

If you think I'm going to help you remember her name, you're way offside, Larry thought grimly. You've got to remember her on your own.

"She was a wonderful person," Paul Mitchell went on

softly. "Her name was Martha Donnell . . ." His voice trailed off and he looked at Larry uncertainly. "Have I done something wrong?"

"Not yet, you haven't," Larry told him. "But unless you get yourself over to her house right away, you will."

Paul Mitchell looked startled at first, and then gradually that expression gave way to a broad grin. He turned to leave the room, and just at the door he said, "Good-by, and thank you."

Well, Martha Donnell told herself firmly: The best thing for you to do, friend, is to get busy. Very busy. Or else. I'll clean the kitchen, she thought, answering her own ultimatum.

That was the job she hated most, and therefore the one most calculated to keep her from thinking. The weather was much too nice for thinking. If she let her mind go free, it went whirling off in all sorts of unprofitable directions— such as why she couldn't say yes to Andrew Fowler, who was such a nice man. What if he did have an oversized Adam's apple and a voice that sounded like a squeaking gate hinge? He had money, didn't he? And he was sober and kind and passed the plate at church and would be good to Clark. . . .

Because I can't endure the sight of him, that's why, she told herself fiercely. And what are you looking for? her troublesome other self demanded, sensibly enough.

"I'm looking for . . ." she began, and then realized she had spoken the words out loud and that, even worse, she was about to add a description of the man she was looking for. It wasn't Andy Fowler at all, but a very real man, not a dream. His face came clear to her, and the sound of his voice, not at all like a gate hinge. She stopped just short of saying his name. That was when she decided she'd better clean the kitchen.

Her first impulse was to change her dress, for it was still fairly new and would do to wear to school for several seasons if she took care of it. Instead, not wanting to let herself be distracted from her purpose, she went straight to the kitchen.

Once there, she crawled up on the sink drainboard in order to reach the glass jars stored on the top shelf. She removed each one and set it carefully in the sink. Pretty soon there was a smudge of dust across her nose, her hands were grimy and her hair had come loose from its pins. She realized she must look like a pioneer woman after six months on the trail. Why did she keep all these empty jars, anyway? She had a positive mania about them. Why didn't she throw them away, instead of storing them on a top shelf against the day they might be needed and then, at housecleaning time, washing them carefully and putting them back?

Across the street on the vacant lot, a group of children shouted as they played baseball—or, at least, their version of it. Clark was with them, having as good a time as anyone. "Throw it," she heard one of them yell. "You goon—*throw it!*"

She looked at the small glass jar in her hand. She looked at the wastebasket in the corner.

"Throw it!" The yell was truly urgent now.

Bang! The jar hit the wastebasket. She jumped at the noise it made and gasped. She hadn't really . . .

Oh, yes, she had. The sight of the broken jar lying in the wastebasket seemed to release something within her. She reached for a second one.

Bang! And then, *bang, bang, bang!*

There was an imposing heap of broken glass in the wastebasket and only a few jars left on the shelf when a knock came on the front door. A neighbor, no doubt, wanting to know if she had lost her mind.

"Come in," she ordered belligerently. "I'm in the kitchen."

There was a moment of hesitancy on the part of the caller, and then she heard the screen door open and footsteps coming through the living room, into the dining room, and then at last to the kitchen doorway. She turned, and there stood Paul Mitchell.

"Oh!" she gasped. Her hand flew to her hair, although she knew all she got for her gesture was some extra dust on her nose. "Paul."

"Hello," he said diffidently.

"So you *did* come back," she said and felt her face burning through its coating of dust. "I—I'm cleaning house," she explained inanely.

He had come back after having been away for months, and here she was perched on the drainboard looking like a fugitive from a rummage sale, unable to say anything that resembled sense.

"Yes, I'm back," he told her softly. "Here—let me help you down."

In a moment she was standing beside him in the middle of the kitchen. "It's good to see you," she said primly.

They stood there, looking at each other. He was thinner, she noticed above her own confusion, but he looked better, healthier, in some way that she could not immediately define.

"You're just the way I remember you," he said.

Oh, no, she thought. Surely he didn't remember her like this!

"After the operation, those weeks I was in the hospital, I'd wake up nights and wonder if I had only dreamed of you. I thought maybe you weren't here at all—not in Benson, anyway. But you are here."

"Yes, I'm here," she said softly. Suddenly it didn't matter how she looked.

"You know about me?" he asked.

"Oh, yes," she told him hurriedly.

She wasn't going to make him repeat the details. She knew the whole story.

"There's so much I have to catch up on," he told her. "I mean, there are gaps in my memory. Some things come back clearly, but sometimes I have to figure out whether they really happened or whether I dreamed them. By the way, how's Clark? That's his name, isn't it? Your nephew?"

"He's fine," she said, oddly disappointed.

"I thought I remembered him, really, that is," Paul Mitchell said. He moved closer to her, regarding her with a scrutiny both exciting and disconcerting. "Tell me something," he said.

He hesitated a long time, and finally she prompted him impatiently. "Yes?"

He cleared his throat. "Did I—did I kiss you once?"

Martha let out her breath quickly, trying not to laugh. Suddenly it was all very funny—beautifully, deliciously funny. She felt a wild urge to giggle. "You did," she said, "and then walked out on me. Just like that."

"I *knew* it," he said. "I knew that was real. I kept telling myself it was. That was one of the reasons I had to come back—to find out I wasn't mistaken about it. And about you."

He reached out to take her hand, slowly, giving her time to pull away if she wanted to. She stood quietly, her hand in his, feeling herself begin to tremble.

"You say you know, so there's no need going over it all. I'm told the papers covered the story pretty thoroughly."

"Yes," she said. "But we never blamed you. Nobody did."

"But I was responsible for the wreck. I was the one driving —don't forget that. Those two children died because of me."

"Four of them lived because of you," she reminded him. "Just remember, everyone has something in his life he wishes he could change. We just have to go on from where we are."

He smiled at her, warmth and tenderness in his eyes.

"Shall we—" He hesitated, as if seeking the courage to go on. Then apparently he found it, for he said, "Shall we go on from where we left off?"

Her answer must have shown in her expression, for he put his arms around her, drawing her close, and bent toward her. For a second she found herself wondering if he could find a clean spot on her face. Then she forgot all about it, for he had kissed her.

"You're real, all right," he whispered. "It's all real."

And it was. Real and wonderful.

The Voyager

FOR THIRTY YEARS MISS GOLDIE PARKS TAUGHT SIXTH-GRADE geography in Tyson, Texas. Nine months of each year she looked out of the same classroom windows, and what she saw was sameness. For the town was set in a great monotony of spaces, a vastness of sky and flat land and meager vegetation, broken occasionally by arroyos down which flash floods sometimes poured—roaring, tawny menaces on their way to join the Rio Grande.

When vacation came, Miss Goldie was as anxious to get away as were any of her pupils. Then, it was, she took her trips.

"Where are you going this summer, Miss Goldie?" we would ask.

"First I must go see my mother, who isn't well." She always went first to see her mother who "wasn't well." "And after that—well, I don't know. But I'll bring you back pictures and things."

She did. She brought so many pictures and maps and travel folders and other items that she had to hire a drayman to haul them to school for her. It was these things she brought for us to see that made the places she visited come alive for us, too, so that we began to talk about them as if we had been there ourselves. Miss Goldie never spoke of "studying about" a country. She always said we "went there." We picked up the phrase from her.

Miss Goldie was really small, although she gave the impression of being tall. Perhaps that was because she carried herself with an eager vitality, as if always there were a great many things she must do quickly because she was in a hurry to be off somewhere else. Her clothes were utterly without distinction. No matter how hard I try, I cannot remember a single thing she wore.

"She ought to buy herself some decent clothes," Mother said once, "instead of spending all her money on trips."

Of all the names she might have borne, Goldie was the one which fitted her least. Mousie would have been far better, for she was all of a color—eyes, hair, skin blended into a single pattern. I suppose her clothes blended into the pattern also. Certainly the effect was not golden. Taupe would have been the nearer color—that curious in-between shade that retreats apologetically into the back of one's wardrobe.

About Miss Goldie herself, however, there was nothing apologetic. Both in and out of her classroom she moved with an unself-conscious assurance, bearing at the same time a look both remote and alert. Former students remembered her and talked about her long after they forgot other more dynamic, attractive teachers. In fact, I find it hard now to separate the things I actually saw her do from those I merely heard about.

Year after year they came back to see her, these former students, and never once was she known to fumble a name. She remembered them all.

"Hello, Miss Goldie."

"Hello, Tom."

"Say, I saw Yellowstone this summer. It was just like you said it would be."

"Good."

"Where is the class going this semester?"

"Just now we are in China."

"Fine. I think I liked China best of all the places we went." The old phrase fell easily off his lips.

He left, and Miss Goldie turned back to her class.

"Now the Great Wall of China was built for protection," she said.

The class would have almost sworn that she had helped with the construction, so positive was her statement. For they were not merely studying about a wall. They had "gone" there, and in so doing, had made the place their own forever more.

Once this kinship with another land did not come so easily. That was when Jack Benetti entered school.

Jack's mother had been Sylvia Thatcher, a Tyson girl who had gone East to school and there had met and married an Italian named Benetti. Her family gave out that he was a count, but Miss Carrie Fulton said he was more than likely a fruit peddler. (A great many people in Tyson thought Sylvia gave herself airs, a thing unforgivable in that region.) The young couple settled down in New York, and Sylvia never came home for a visit. She had a son, whom she named Jack for her father. The boy was twelve years old when she came back to Tyson to live, bringing him with her. Her husband did not come with her, a matter which she did not feel she needed to explain. Tyson took that rather hard.

Jack entered the sixth grade. He was a small, nervous, over-polite boy with dark coloring and melting brown eyes. From the first, he was a marked character.

"Hey, got any bananas to sell?" the other boys would call. And then they would chant, "Wop—Wop—Wop—"

And then came the day when Jack found himself on the playground facing a line of boys who were armed with sticks and clods. But these were feeble things beside the more cruel weapon they held—a feeling of solidarity among themselves, a fabric held together by the cement of intolerance.

"Go back to Italy—" they yelled.

But their hearts were not quite in the game. This Italian boy was showing courage, and that was a thing to be respected wherever it is found.

"I am an American," Jack said. He was very white, and looked as if he might be sick at any moment. "I was born in New York, and that is America. My father was a naturalized American. Besides, my mother was born here in this town."

He wanted to cry, and did not. That made his tormentors uneasy, and strangely enough, all the more determined to continue their persecution.

Just then Miss Goldie came by, making her rounds of the playground. She gave no indication that she realized she had come upon a scene in which anything was amiss.

"Of course you are an American," she said, as if he were taking part in some game, like spelling the names of capitals. "An American of Italian descent. Nearly all Americans are descended from some other nationality."

The bell rang, and everyone went back to the classrooms.

Scarcely had the children got seated when Miss Goldie, as if she were handing them the earth and most of the planets, said, "Today we are going to Rome." She said it although at that moment there were any number of folders and books on her desk bearing the label "Alaska." "Open your books to page 212," she said, clearing her desk of the piles of material there. "By the time you have finished reading, I'll have some material about Rome on the table. Remember—extra points for all outside material you bring in."

The next day the table well-nigh collapsed with its load of things Roman. The room began to be filled with shaky handiwork—replicas of the Colosseum, and other Roman buildings. There were dolls in togas, sitting in the Senate. Through all this construction and study, Jack Benetti, even more than Miss Goldie, was technical adviser and director. He gave his information with simple dignity and great assurance.

"That's the way it really is," he would say. And then he would turn to Miss Goldie to ask politely, "Isn't it?"

"Indeed it is," she would assure him.

The day after Jack had been chosen first in baseball (where it was discovered he could run faster than any of the other boys) Miss Goldie rolled down the big wall map.

"Today we are going to Italy," she said. And then she added casually, "Rome is in Italy, you know."

So they "went to" Italy. And finally they concluded, quietly egged on by Miss Goldie, that it was rather a proud thing to be Italian.

The case of Jack Benetti might have been an accident. Only it happened much the same way with a tough little red-head the boys began to call "Shanty Irish" before he had more than set foot on the playground, and with the only Jewish lad in town. I think she could have done the same thing for a Hottentot, or a South African, or a Burmese. For she knew the world, had her fingers on its pulsing currents, slipped easily into talk of its people. And we of Tyson, scarcely conscious of what we did, followed her through ever widening horizons.

Perhaps there was not anyone who followed her so completely as did the members of the Travel Club. Somewhere
early in the organization's history, Miss Goldie had been
asked to plan the year's program. After that, the Club program *was* Miss Goldie. She was very firm with the members;
after all, most of them had been her pupils and, in her presence, became once more little girls anxious to get extra grade
points for outside work. She conducted the Club study as
she conducted her classes—with an inspired thoroughness
that made each member feel she "had gone" to the places
studied.

And so it was, when the world went mad, that strange
names like Iwo Jima and Guadalcanal and Saipan did not
send the women of Tyson scuttling to the atlas. This knowledge was not always a good thing. It gave mothers a white-
lipped certainty about the character of the country in which
their boys fought. Perhaps it also explained why Tyson always oversubscribed its Red Cross and War Bond quotas.

On the days Miss Goldie conducted the Club program
there was a sort of glow about her, a thing that transcended
clothes. It was then that her name was not too incongruous.

The war brought a new type of returned student to Miss
Goldie's door. He wore a uniform, and he did not talk of
going to Yellowstone.

"Hello, Miss Goldie. Say, I've been to Japan."

"Hello, Bill. Yes, I knew you went. I read your letters in the paper. Even used them on the bulletin board."

"I hoped you would. That was partly why I wrote them." He blushed a little as he told her.

"I'm glad you kept your eyes open and learned things."

"Yes, ma'am." He was six feet tall, and had three stripes on his sleeve. But before her was a little boy, seeking to prove his worthiness. "Yes, ma'am. I watched the country, and the people. Maybe this will sound funny to you, but we're going to have to learn to get along with those Japs, after this is over."

"We are going to have to learn to get along with people everywhere."

"Say, Miss Goldie," he grinned at her, "do I get extra points for doing those letters?"

"You always do, don't you?" Miss Goldie said dryly. But you could tell she appreciated his joke.

"Funny thing," he said, all seriousness now, "first time I saw Japan I felt like I'd been there before."

The boys of Tyson were to say that same thing in the far reaches of the Pacific, in Africa, in Europe, in Asia—"I'll be dogged if this place don't look familiar. Guess we've 'been here' before with Miss Goldie."

"Not much like Tyson, was it?" Miss Goldie would ask them later.

"Not much. And yet it is, too. Guess it's like you used to

tell us—all people and places are sort of alike, underneath."

The first few months after the war ended, Miss Goldie's door was full of boys most of the time.

"Say, Miss Goldie—I got to Switzerland. You ought to go back there."

"I'll go sometime."

"Why don't you go this summer?"

"I'll think about it—"

The years went by, and more and more young people came to stand at Miss Goldie's door. They came from Germany and Japan and Korea and other far-flung places where American troops were stationed; they had furloughs from oil companies with headquarters in Saudi Arabia; and, in the case of the girls, they returned from summer sessions at the University of Hawaii and from student tours to out-of-the-way spots in the world. Always Miss Goldie listened to them with interest, nodding her head in agreement, giving the impression that she knew, from firsthand experience, that their accounts were correct.

Then came the spring when she won first place in an essay contest, sponsored by the West Texas Chamber of Commerce, on "The Resources of Texas." The prize was an all-expense trip to Austin and the Alamo.

"Just to think," Miss Goldie said, "I've never seen the Alamo, or the capitol."

"Why, Miss Goldie," we protested in shocked unbelief.

She who knew every syllable of their history, she who had been everywhere else, had never seen the two most historic places in her own state.

Wasn't it fortunate, she said, that the trip was scheduled for mid-June. Because of that, she could go by and spend a few days with her mother. "She lives with my married sister, you know."

We didn't. Nobody seemed to know anything at all about her personal life. Even Carrie Fulton, with whom she boarded, knew nothing much.

Her friends gave her a farewell dinner. Miss Goldie thought it very nice of them. Everyone was being nice, she said. Her brother-in-law couldn't meet her bus, but he was leaving the pick-up at the station so she could drive out to the farm the minute she got in.

Her bus was late leaving. There had been big rains to the north, snarling traffic. But finally she got started, sitting stiffly in the window seat, wearing her no-colored dress with a no-colored coat over it. She waved debonairly at those down to see her off.

"I declare," Carrie Fulton said, "she looked for the world and all like someone sailing away on a big liner."

And that was the last anyone in Tyson saw of her.

Carrie Fulton, one of the last to see her, was the first one to have the news. The brother-in-law called her, and the news he had to relate sent her, tears streaming down her face, to our house.

"The most horrible thing has happened," she said. "Miss Goldie Parks has been drowned—"

Mother said, "Oh no—" and the way she said it, I knew she felt as I did. Not Miss Goldie. She was eternal, everlasting—like the mountains she taught us about.

"It was a flash flood," Carrie went on. "She got caught in the arroyo that runs between her sister's house and town. They found the truck, but they haven't found her. They've given up hope by now. More than likely her body is down to the Rio Grande—maybe even on its way to the sea—"

"Poor Miss Goldie," Mother said. "She didn't get her trip. But then," she added quickly, "she's had so many trips—"

"That's where you're wrong," Carrie said. "I found out from her brother-in-law. She'd never had a trip. Never, in all her life."

The town had her story now, a story as fantastic as the news of her death. Miss Goldie had never been anywhere, save to her sister's to nurse the mother who "was not well." Every summer she spent there.

It was during these summer months that she "took" her trips. She had her mail sent there—travel folders, books, advertisements, magazines. She read these, and for that time, she literally lived in the country about which she studied. Here she traced the routes of her "travel" which she brought back to us. They were the fabric from which romance was made, and when she shared them with us, they were real for us, too. Who were we to say she had deceived us?

We talked it over uncertainly.

"She never *really* said she went to those places—I mean, really *went* there, did she?"

"Well, no. Remember—she called it 'going to' a place when we studied it."

Yes, we remembered.

We remembered, and we could not feel sad. It was as if one of Miss Goldie's wall maps had unrolled, letting us see the true picture of the thing that had happened to her; as if all the wisdom she had given us about far places was crystallizing into a single moment of perception. She had given us a kinship with space, a feeling of being at one with the universe. And we followed her now in the path she had prepared for us.

We knew, at last, Miss Goldie had embarked upon a Journey Magnificent. And, as always, the old magic held.

Thanks to Aunt Millicent

IT WAS THE FALL AFTER MY UNCLE HORACE MARRIED AUNT Millicent that Mother began to worry about my health. I was twelve years old at the time, shaped like a meal sack and never sick. Perhaps it was because Mother had had no experience with ailing children that she let my condition run on an entire winter and well into the next summer without taking any definite steps about it. Or perhaps it was because, in common with everyone else in town, she was too preoccupied with Uncle Horace's new wife to give anything else a thought.

My Uncle Horace was a big man and very handsome. He liked spirited horses, gay parties with the "Fast Set," and fishing trips from which he brought back neither fish nor alibis for not having them. And he had a way with women. You could work your way up and down the town from Main Street to the edge, both ways, and hardly find a home where some woman wasn't eating her heart out for Uncle

Horace. In fact, though Mother and Father took pains to hide it from my ears, I knew that Uncle Horace came as near as anyone in town to leading what Brother Sneed called, threateningly and vaguely, "a life of sin."

I don't know whether he was really wild, or whether they just couldn't tell which way he was going to jell—into a respectable businessman who would settle down to help his brother (my father) in their store, or into a gay old dog who would embarrass his family. Now that he was nearing thirty, with no mending of his ways, I think more and more people were leaning to the latter view.

And then, while he was away from town on one of his frequent and unexplained trips, the telegram came back saying he would bring his bride home the following Saturday.

You never saw such a commotion in town since the time Deacon Billings' son tried to rob the First National Bank. People met in little groups to discuss the marriage. Sidewalk loafers laid bets on how long it would last, the most optimistic giving it a year. Three young ladies took to their beds with sick headaches. Two more left town to visit friends. The band began practicing suitable numbers to play as the train bearing the newlyweds pulled in, and the mayor appointed a reception committee. For in spite of his wild ways—or maybe because of them—there was no more popular person in town than my Uncle Horace.

Thanks to Aunt Millicent

Mother began her own special preparations. All her best Haviland came out, and I was put to polishing silver and cut glass. In the dining room the huge claw-legged table was pulled to a length usually reserved for Christmas and Thanksgiving.

Mother did not go to the station to join the townspeople in welcoming the bride and groom. Nor did she allow me to go. She gave as her excuse the dinner that needed her last-minute attention. But she didn't fool me a minute's worth. She couldn't be sure just what kind of a woman was going to step off that train, and if she had to be humiliated, she preferred having it happen right here in her own home, with her own china and silver and coconut layer cake behind her to give her strength to bear it.

So we fiddled around, doing those things which well might have been left undone, until we saw Uncle Horace's buggy driving into the gate. He sat very straight, and he seemed to be holding in check his restless energy. You could tell it by the steady look around his mouth and the way he had black Nero reined in. And when he helped the woman at his side out of the buggy, he did it as if she were a precious piece of china.

Whatever we expected Uncle Horace's new wife to be like, it was certainly not Aunt Millicent. The first thing you thought of when you saw her was how small she was and how frail. It was a hard thing to understand for really she was taller than my mother. But frail she was, with a frailness that had a sort of negative quality. She was not sick, or bedfast, or in pain. She was just "not strong," a fact to which she referred seldom, and then only with apology. She did not need to mention it. Everything about her—her clothes, her white, transparent skin, her delicate, small-boned hands, her gentle voice—gave the impression that here was a woman whose hold on life was none too sure.

It was a quality that seemed to draw people to her. It had drawn Uncle Horace, where the charms of more buxom, vivacious, and determined women had failed. And now it drew my mother.

"My dear," she cried, putting her arms around her new sister-in-law, "you must come in and have a good rest before supper. You look utterly worn out!"

The next day was Sunday, which had always meant going to church, and no nonsense about it. That is, it did for everyone but Uncle Horace.

On those rare week ends which he spent in town, he often came to our house. He liked Mother and was never cross when she begged him to put aside his wild ways and settle down. He would sit there, laughing at her and teasing her while he ate her good bread and jam and drank her excellent coffee. Seldom did he think of getting up before noon on Sunday.

Thanks to Aunt Millicent

We had expected that this Sunday morning would be no different from all the others. So, when we heard footsteps in the hall, Mother was so flustered she upset her cup of coffee right on the table. She was busy mopping it up when the door opened, and in walked Uncle Horace and Aunt Millicent.

Uncle Horace looked sleepy, but Aunt Millicent was too lovely for words. She was wearing a lacy thing called a wrapper, with ribbons at the throat.

"If I had known you were getting up . . ." Mother began.

"Please don't bother about us," Aunt Millicent said. "We don't want much, and we'll eat here with you. We mustn't be late for church. You'll have to hurry, Horace. You're not nearly ready."

"I didn't plan to go," Uncle Horace told her casually, "I thought I'd just stay here and have dinner ready for you."

Now that was a joke. Anything funnier than Uncle Horace cooking a meal could not well be imagined.

"Of course," Aunt Millicent said gently, "I could go without you, but I'd feel so lonely and strange this first time. I wouldn't mind so much, only I'm feeling dizzy this morning."

"I wouldn't think of letting you go alone, dear," Uncle Horace said, "I'll get ready right away."

You could fairly feel the gasp that followed him as he went down the aisle with Aunt Millicent hanging on his arm. She looked like something out of a picture book. Seeing her, the choir lost its place and Brother Sneed dropped his nose glasses to the floor. If Uncle Horace was aware of these things, he gave no sign. And during the service he fanned her carefully. Once I heard him ask her something about feeling the heat, and she shook her head, smiling so sweetly at him that little prickles ran up and down my hands and arms like they did when I read those lovely novels I was not supposed to.

After services, everyone crowded around the newly married couple. They wanted, so they said, to see what kind of a woman would be willing to put up with Old Horace.

Aunt Millicent was lovely and gracious to everyone— the people who joked and the ones who offered their good wishes with proper sobriety. Mother was as proud as Uncle Horace.

At Aunt Millicent's invitation, I rode home in the buggy with her and Uncle Horace. The trip was not unmixed with bitterness. The pride I felt at being asked was overlaid with a strange kind of misery. Up until now I had known a healthy disregard for my apple-dumpling figure, the plain clothes Mother thought suitable for a tomboy like me, my straight, black hair and freckled nose. Now, pressed close to Aunt Millicent's lace and ruffles, I was suddenly aware of my square heaviness, my plain print dress, my sturdy shoes. For the first time in my life I was aware of my appearance and I was acutely unhappy.

The unhappiness still sat heavily on me when Mother called us to dinner. And when Father began heaping my plate, I said I didn't want anything. Mother asked if I were sick, and I said yes, I was. Sickness was as good a name as any for the lump that had settled between my stomach and my throat. After dinner I was bundled off to bed, along with Aunt Millicent, who kept protesting that she was perfectly all right and there was no reason in the world for coddling her. But Uncle Horace said she looked simply worn out, that going to church had done it, and next Sunday she wasn't going a step.

But she did go. It was Uncle Horace who stayed at home. During that week they had moved into Grandmother Gaynor's house, the one she had left to Uncle Horace when she died. It was a lovely house and Aunt Millicent said so, too. Only, she said gently, there were a great many changes that would have to be made. Uncle Horace said he didn't see any reason for changing things.

But they made a number of them, even that first week, so on Sunday Uncle Horace said he was too tired to go to church, and just rolled over and went back to sleep when Aunt Millicent called him. She telephoned to ask if we would take her to church. She didn't blame poor Horace for being too worn out to go. She was exhausted herself.

"You shouldn't be going yourself," Mother protested

when we stopped for her, "you look worn out."

Aunt Millicent said nonsense. It was just the heat, and the hard week she had had, and her disappointment at Horace's not going. She always felt bad when she was disappointed. It was childish of her, and she was trying to overcome it. Only, she had set her heart on having dear Horace go to church with her every single Sunday. There was nothing that held a man and woman together like regular church attendance.

The very bird on Mother's hat took a triumphant angle. She said dear Millicent was right, but she need have no worries about holding Horace.

And Aunt Millicent said it made her happy to hear dear Sadie say that, especially when she knew no one expected she could.

When we went down the aisle you could feel a chuckle going up all over the church. So good Old Horace had stayed at home, had he—just what everyone expected!

Aunt Millicent sat through the services, taking part just as if her husband were there holding the book for her. Not so many crowded around her as on the Sunday before, but there were plenty of witnesses when she gave a little gasp and crumpled up at Father's feet.

Father picked her up and laid her on a church bench. Everybody told everybody else to stand back and give her air. Somebody sent several people running for water. Mother chafed her hands and fanned her, and by and by Aunt Millicent's eyes began to open. Pretty soon she sat up and said weakly that she was all right. But Father said she looked like a sick kitten. He carried her to the carriage himself, while all the time she said she was perfectly able to walk. Mother and I sat on either side of her, and Father drove the horses too fast for such a hot day. Every once in awhile he'd turn back to ask if she were feeling all right. But just before we drove up to her house, she seemed to have a sort of relapse.

Even now I don't like to remember the look on Uncle Horace's face when my father came into the house, carrying Aunt Millicent in his arms.

"Millicent," he cried.

"It's nothing," Aunt Millicent protested weakly, "just the heat . . ."

Uncle Horace was no good at all. It was Mother who took charge.

"Now, Tom," she said, "you go for Dr. Fenton, and, Horace, you help me get her to bed."

By the time Dr. Fenton got there Aunt Millicent was in bed. She tried to tell him she was perfectly all right, and it was foolish for them to trouble him. He plunked down his bag, went over to her and took one of her little hands in his.

"So this is Horace's new wife," he said heartily. "What's

the matter—hasn't he been feeding you enough?"

For once in his life Uncle Horace didn't have a word to say. You could see he was thinking his wife was going to die, maybe, and he hadn't gone to church when she asked him.

Doc Fenton went over Aunt Millicent carefully. He made her stick out her tongue and listened to her heart. When he finally took the rubber thing off his ears he looked at her queerly.

"Yes," he said, "yes, I think it's just the heat. Take it easy a day or two. I'll send you a tonic."

And then he turned to me.

"How are you, young lady," he laughed, "appetite failing?"

He laughed because he knew my appetite was one thing that never failed. But I couldn't laugh with him. Suddenly I knew I was going to be sick—very sick. I suppose it must have been the excitement and the heat. I put my pudgy hand over my mouth and ran from the room.

Doc Fenton and Mother came on my heels.

"What ails the child, Sadie?" he rumbled. "Been up another apple tree?"

Mother said, not that she knew of, but I probably needed a good dose of calomel, and did he have any.

He did, and beg as I would, Mother gave me a Spartan dose. I went to bed, too sick to care whether I wore my best nightgown, even though Mother said I might.

By the next day the medicine had done its work and I was well again. But it was the middle of the week before Aunt Millicent was able to be up. By Sunday she was quite herself and she and Uncle Horace went to church with him watching her like she couldn't even get her breath without him there to help her. After that he never missed a Sunday from church.

Aunt Millicent threw herself into church work right away. She never spared herself, although everyone could see she was ready to drop lots of times. Pretty soon all the church women were watching out for her the way Mother and Uncle Horace did.

"She just won't spare herself," Mother said to Father, "and with her heart like it is . . ."

"Did Doc Fenton say it was her heart?" Father asked.

"Well, no. He doesn't act as if there's anything much wrong with her. But you know how he is. I declare, I sometimes think I'd have to be half-dead before he'd do anything for me. I sort of got it from Millicent. Oh, she didn't say it in so many words, for the poor darling doesn't want Horace to worry. But I've seen heart cases before."

"And, of course," Father grinned, "you've not said a single word to Horace!"

"Well," Mother dimpled, "you know how it is. I figured it wouldn't hurt Horace a bit to know his wife wasn't strong. It gives a man a feeling of responsibility."

"I can't see that it's hurt me any to have a strong, well wife," Father said stoutly, "and I'll be dogged if I think it could hurt Horace."

"Oh," Mother's voice was a shocked whisper, "but that is different!"

Father maintained stoutly that he couldn't see the difference, and Mother was determined that he should, and so they fell into one of their rare quarrels until at last Father had to admit what everybody in town was admitting, that Horace's wife had him right under her thumb, something nobody thought any woman could ever do.

I guess the women who had been in love with Uncle Horace were the last ones to believe he had eyes only for his wife. But Aunt Millicent was very broad-minded about them. She would single them out, go and sit by them, and talk to them and encourage them to talk to her. And somehow they always seemed suddenly to look blowzy, and they would talk loud and laugh too much. By the side of Aunt Millicent's fragile daintiness, they seemed coarse and common.

Only once do I remember that Uncle Horace neglected Aunt Millicent in public and that was the night of the oyster supper when he was quite attentive to the new schoolteacher. It didn't last long, though, for Aunt Millicent confessed that she had not been feeling well all day and that she'd just slip off now. Tom would take her. Dear Horace was having too good a time to be disturbed. But Uncle Horace found out and took her home himself. And as they left the new teacher said something under her breath that made the people around her laugh a lot.

I didn't know what it was, but Mother was furious. Probably it had something to do with the teacher's failure to be reelected the next year, what with Mother feeling the way she did and Father being on the board. But Mother's pleasure at the way Uncle Horace had behaved when he found his wife was ill almost made up for her anger at the teacher.

"Horace didn't hesitate a minute," she said triumphantly to Father. "He took her right home. Every day he is developing into a better man and a better husband. And maybe . . ."

She gave him the look that was as close as she ever got to mentioning babies before they were born.

"Anything like that in the wind yet?" Father asked.

Mother had to admit that there wasn't, as far as she knew. But dear Millicent had been feeling wretched all week, and perhaps . . .

"Couldn't be because Horace had talked about going over to Everly on business, could it?" Father asked.

"Tom Fulton," Mother cried, "I'm ashamed of you. You know how much Millicent has done for Horace. Her frailness has brought out the best in him. He's a new man, and you know it."

"Well, maybe," Father said, "but I wouldn't bet too much on it until the fishing season is over."

Mother said that was nonsense, but I knew she was worried about the fishing season, too. Those trips of Uncle Horace's had been open scandals for years. They were the sort of thing men laughed a great deal about, and women discussed in horrified whispers.

Mother was so worried about it that she didn't have time to pay much attention to me. I was thinner, and I had no appetite at all. Instead of going outdoors and climbing trees, I stayed in the house and looked in the glass, and moped over what I saw. No matter how thin I got, I didn't look the least like Aunt Millicent. I kept at Mother until she made me a pale blue dress, all trimmed in lace, and when I put it on I looked awful.

Dr. Fenton said it was my age, and to give me a dose of sulphur and molasses. I took it, and it didn't help a bit. Before Mother could ask him about another dose, he had left town because his daughter up North was very sick. And then something happened that put Mother in such a fizz, she wouldn't have known if I had practically fallen dead at her feet.

Uncle Horace said he was going on a fishing trip. He made the announcement casually, while he and Aunt Millicent were eating Sunday dinner at our house. "I plan to leave Tuesday," he said. "Bunch of fellows going up to Elbow Lake. Fishing ought to be pretty good now."

Aunt Millicent got very pale around the mouth, but she was the one who found her voice first. And she said sweetly she was glad dear Horace could go away and enjoy himself. He hadn't had a vacation in such a long time. She'd help him get ready tomorrow. And now if Sadie would excuse her, she'd go and lie down. No, she didn't want any dessert, but the rest of us might go right on with ours.

I was pretty thrilled when Mother told me Monday morning that I was to go over and see if I could help Aunt Millicent. I still got goose bumps, every time I came near her. She always looked so nice and smelled like violets.

It was very quiet when I got to Aunt Millicent's. I decided she must be lying down, so I slipped around to the kitchen so Maisie could let me in. I was very careful to keep on the walk, for the flower beds had been watered that morning—Uncle Horace took good care of Aunt Millicent's flowers.

I didn't see a thing of Maisie. But through the window I did see Aunt Millicent. She was standing on a chair, reaching up to the closet. On the floor were lying Uncle Horace's fishing things—his tackle, the old hamper with the cooking things in it, and the bag in which he carried his clothes. I had never seen Aunt Millicent make anything but languid gestures, but now she was twisting about, quick as a bird. And though Uncle Horace wouldn't let her lift anything heavier than a pocket handkerchief, she was tossing about that fishing equipment with as much energy as Mother used in spring cleaning. While I stood watching her with my mouth wide open, she piled all the things back on the shelf. This time she sort of pulled things out, letting them fall where they would. Then she got off her chair again, and got down on the floor, with all the bags and things, and lay down.

She did it several times, moving things about and lying down each time to test the new grouping. Only it wasn't lying so much as just sort of flowing.

I forgot what I was doing, watching her, and stepped off the walk, into the flower bed, in mud ankle deep. And my one concern was to sneak away before Aunt Millicent saw me.

Mother was that cross with me, once I got home. She said I could just clean myself up and get into a nightgown and go to bed. She'd go herself to help Aunt Millicent. I tried to tell her Aunt Millicent didn't need help but Mother wouldn't listen to me. And I was feeling pretty sorry for myself, when they came screaming for Mother to come quick —Aunt Millicent was dying.

Mother and I ran the five blocks that separated the two

houses, and we had come to Aunt Millicent's front door before either of us noticed I was still in my nightgown. But
there was such bedlam going on in that house that nobody
would have known if I hadn't worn a stitch. Of course the
doctor was out of town, but the neighbors were there. And
Uncle Horace was acting like a mad man.

"She's dying, Sadie," he told Mother when he met us at
the door.

"Where is she," Mother asked, "and what happened?"

"She's in the back storeroom," he said. "She was getting
my fishing things out of the closet, and she collapsed, right
there in the middle of them. I wouldn't dare try to move
her until you came. But if she dies, Sadie, it's my fault . . ."
His voice broke.

"There, there," Mother said soothingly and followed him
to the room where Aunt Millicent lay.

Sure enough, there she was, among the fishing things. She
had on a white lacy wrapper, the one she had worn that
morning, months ago, when they had eaten breakfast in
our kitchen. Her hair was hanging loose about her face. She
was pale, and she lay so quietly it was hard to tell if she
was breathing. I had never seen her look more beautiful.

Only, all I could think of was that she was lying exactly
the way I had seen her not more than half an hour ago.
I was opening my mouth to tell Uncle Horace not to worry
—that she had been lying just like that and then had got up

and put all the fishing things back once before this morning—when she opened her eyes.

"Horace," she cried, stretching out her hands, "darling, you've come. But you shouldn't have, I'm perfectly all right . . ."

"Millicent," he cried, "you're all right. Listen, darling, I'm not going fishing, so help me God," and his voice sounded like somebody joining the church or getting married, "I'm never going to leave you again, never, as long as I live."

I shut my mouth tight. And I kept it shut all the time Aunt Millicent kept protesting that he might go right on and take his trip. I kept it shut that evening when Mother told Father all about dear Millicent's terrible spell. I even kept it shut, years afterward, when everyone was marveling how a frail, little thing like Aunt Millicent could outlive Old Horace, who had always been as strong as an ox.

Most of all I kept it shut when Mother said she couldn't understand what on earth had changed me overnight from a child who was sick half the time into a girl who wouldn't admit she was hurt, even if a barn fell over on her.

The New House

WHENEVER MYRA CONSIDERED THE MATTER AT ALL, SHE KNEW
she had not fallen in love with Dick. She had grown into
love. It was only the discovery that was sudden and, once
having made it, she knew she would never be free of loving
him, never again be unaware of him.

At the time it happened, they were both working for Hill
and Harte, architects—he as junior partner, she as secretary. He wasn't at all the type of man she admired. For
one thing, he was short, only a few inches taller than she
was, really. She liked tall lean men. Besides that, he was
quiet and serious. Myra wanted to go with a man who would
take her to dances and send her flowers and tell her she
looked wonderful. She supposed it was silly and flighty of
her but she liked men that were *fun*.

Dick Branson was good and quiet and steady and dependable, but not fun. He and his father lived together.
His mother was dead. That was about all she knew of his
personal life.

He was nice to work with, though—considerate and un-

189

derstanding and helpful. He had a way of covering up the mistakes she made, both in the work she did for the senior members of the firm and in that which she did for him. This always seemed to link the two of them together in an innocent conspiracy, all the more fun because neither of them ever mentioned it. Whenever she did not know exactly what to do—and these times were not infrequent, for this was her first job—she would turn to him for advice. But outside of the office she scarcely saw him.

He was always apologetic when she had to stay overtime to help him. At such times he usually offered to take her to dinner afterward, but oftener than not she had a date and refused. When she did go with him it was very impersonal, yet friendly. She never felt the least bit self-conscious around him.

That was the way things stood between them one day in mid-May when Dick asked her if she minded staying to finish up some letters. She did mind, but that she did not tell him.

The day was unseasonably warm. She had taken off the coat to her suit; her blouse was rumpled, her hair untidy. She had not had time to powder her nose all afternoon. She had never felt less attractive.

"There, that's done," she said when she had finished. She stood up, stretched her hands above her head. And then it happened.

Dick came to her as she stood there, still with her arms lifted. He put his own arms around her, pulled her to him with a clasp that was both strong and sure.

Her first impulse was to push away from him. That was the right technique—pushing back, laughing a little, ducking just out of reach. If you were interested, you made a good act of drawing away. If you were not, you were kind and gentle—but firm. You couldn't afford to hurt a nice man's feelings, especially if he was your boss. You'd have to work with him afterward and you didn't want any embarrassment on either his or your part.

That was what she should do. But she knew the strangest feeling, standing there in Dick's arms. She didn't want to dodge. She didn't even want to move. It was as if, after long wanderings, she had at last come home. As if she were a kaleidoscope which had been picked up by a master hand, causing all the hundreds of unrelated pieces of her life to fall into a pattern of beauty and rightness.

So, instead of drawing back, she dropped her arms around his neck and relaxed against him. It was then that he kissed her.

It was as natural as breathing, as right as sunlight. She forgot her mussed blouse, her untidy hair, the sticky heat of the day. He kissed her again. She thought fleetingly that she shouldn't completely give up when a man kissed her the first time.

"Myra," he was saying now, a kind of honest male urgency about him, at once both demanding and controlled, "Myra—will you marry me?"

Her answer seemed not to be of her own volition at all; rather, it came from some deep sureness within her.

"Yes," she said. "Oh, yes, darling."

They were married two months later. It was right and wonderful, natural and uncomplicated. She, who had always thought the way to hold a man was to keep him guessing, found that she had no more wish to make Dick unsure of her thoughts than she did to keep her hands or her feet uncertain of her intentions. And Dick seemed to know what she was thinking even before she was aware of it herself.

They got a small apartment and she kept her job. Just as soon as they could afford it, however, they were going to build their own house. She and Dick worked together over the plans. It was a Spanish-type house, with a sunken living room and a blue door. Father Branson thought this an excellent idea. He said a young couple was drawn more closely together when they owned their own home. He was such a quiet gentle person that Myra didn't argue with him but she was thinking that she and Dick couldn't have been any closer.

She sometimes wondered what her life would have been like if Dick hadn't grabbed her and kissed her that afternoon at the office. Before that, she had scarcely noticed him, as a man; after that, he was all of reality, all of love.

They were working on the house plans one October evening when the news came in over the radio. Mr. Harte had died quite suddenly. It was not necessary to put into words the thought which came to both of them. Mr. Harte had been the real power in the firm. With him gone, Hill and Harte would be only a shadow of itself if, indeed, it could survive at all. They knew, too, without discussing the matter overmuch, that two courses were open to Dick. He could stay on, working with Mr. Hill, or he could go looking for another job. In either case, the Spanish house would have to wait for a while.

They talked it over and agreed that the best thing would be for Dick to remain with the firm. This he did, the firm becoming Hill and Branson. For a while, the situation was even more difficult than had been anticipated. Father Branson, undoubtedly suspecting the need for economy on the part of the young people, suggested that they move in with him. He was lonely and wanted them, he said. It was an offer which they gladly accepted.

The Branson house wasn't old but it wasn't new. It had no special distinction about it; it was just a house. There was a large living room with a fireplace that burned real wood and had built-in bookshelves on both sides of it.

There were half-pillars between the living room and the dining room. The woodwork was oak, dark and not very pretty. The kitchen was old-fashioned and inconvenient. The dining room had a bay window that faced east, looking out over a yard filled with trees and flowers and shrubs. A basement housed the furnace and a sort of junk room. There was a back porch that could have been converted into a service room but, since it wasn't, it remained just something to sweep off. There was one bedroom downstairs and two upstairs. The house was painted yellow, the color Myra liked least of all. But it really had a welcoming, gracious air about it, in spite of all these drawbacks. And they told each other that it would do fine.

Living with Father Branson was not difficult at all. He was rather sweet, gentle and quiet and understanding. Because he was so lonesome for his wife, however, he stayed with Myra and Dick more than he might have done under other circumstances. Myra was naturally impulsive and not a little sentimental. She wanted to run to the door evenings and meet Dick, throw herself into his arms. She liked to run across the room and kiss him or rumple his hair or sit on his lap. She was a great one for bestowing silly pet names, not even above breaking into baby talk occasionally.

But in the presence of Dick's father, she hesitated to do any of these things—partly because he was so dignified and reserved, partly because she felt such actions on her part would make him feel in the way. So she put on a quiet dignity that was not hers by nature. At first this was a difficult thing to do. Later she did not find it so hard. And then she came to see that this self-control on her part brought its own reward. Because of it she felt that her love and Dick's took on the quality of an underground stream— all the deeper and surer and more undisturbed because it remained out of sight.

They had been married almost two years when Myra knew she was going to have a baby. Dick insisted that she give up her job immediately, which she did. She felt a small and secret delight in the prospect of staying at home.

The baby was born in May. He was a boy, so of course they named him for his father, calling him Rickie.

The doctor told Myra she should not climb stairs for at least six weeks. Myra hesitated mentioning this to Father Branson, who had the one downstairs bedroom. So, instead, they put up a studio couch in the dining room. There was plenty of room for it and for all the baby paraphernalia as well. These she put in the bay window, through which the morning sun streamed, making the room cheerful and bright.

Myra was entranced with her baby. She loved him because he was hers, because she had brought him into the

world in an agony that had, at the same time, a strange
quality of ecstasy. And because, from the first, he was Dick
in miniature. She would have spoiled him, adoringly and
completely, had not the quiet dignity and self-control of
Dick's father made her feel slightly silly when she gave way
to her temptation to do so. Then Dick, too, restrained her.
So the two men stood between her and her son, injecting
a saving male toughness and strength into her feminine ad-
oration. As the weeks went by, she began to feel she liked
things better so.

At the end of six weeks she went back to the upstairs
bedroom but they did not take the couch out of the dining
room. It seemed comfortable and right there—a good place
to put Rickie for his naps, a good place for her to snatch a
cat nap herself.

It was still there three years later when Betsy was born.

Just as Rickie had been like Dick, now she could see herself in Betsy. The child had about her a certain quicksilver
gaiety. She laughed early and often. Once she began to
talk, she chattered constantly. She was quickly impulsive,
carelessly kind. But for all her light thoughtlessness, she
had a great capacity for tenderness and love . . .

The years slipped by. Without any warning at all, it
seemed, Betsy was a pig-tailed nine and Rickie was twelve.
The couch was still in the dining room; by now, Myra

scarcely noticed it at all save to be grateful for it when she dropped down, exhausted, for a quick nap while the children played in the yard. The house itself had scarcely been changed.

They had got around to screening in the back porch and making an outdoor living room of it. They put a shower in the basement and converted the junk room into a workshop. Here Father Branson taught Rickie to use tools and taught him, as well, the patience and quietness that comes with using one's hands creatively.

Rickie was slight and not tall; he had inherited Dick's build.

"I guess nobody but the big fellows get to play football, do they, Grandpa?" he said wistfully.

"Usually, they are big. But football is not the only game. Ever think of basketball?"

Together they made a basketball goal in the workshop; together they nailed it to the back of the house. Father Branson bought a basketball, set the boy to practicing. Rickie got so he could sink the ball through the basket oftener than he missed it. The attainment of his skill, however, was slow. Myra thought sometimes that she would go crazy if he hit the house one more time with that ball.

Because of the basket on the house, the boys came to the Branson yard to play. They all took turns shooting goals;

they tramped down the basement steps to look at work in progress in the shop; they tracked up her kitchen floor, coming in for drinks. Seeing this, Father Branson rigged up a drinking fountain in the basement. That helped a lot.

He also put a swing and a horizontal bar in the elm tree. These were for Betsy. The girl was as agile and active as a cat and as unself-conscious. She would swing from the bar by her knees, her white petticoat and print dress falling down over her head, her little body naked at the waist, her ruffled white pants totally exposed.

"Lookit me," she would scream to the yard full of goal-shooting boys, while Myra stood inside watching her, wondering what would be the best way to tell her that girls did not hang upside down in the presence of boys.

Dick was no help at all. He was in the garden, his pipe in his mouth, his hands sure and deft with seeds and bulbs and cuttings. Looking at him now, she could see how small the problem really was.

"Betsy," she called, "why don't you come in here and help me make some lemonade?"

It worked. Betsy swung down.

On rainy days the children played inside, either in the basement or in the dining room. They popped corn, made candy, played games on the dining-room table. The house was a mess all the time. Sometimes Myra found herself wishing that the whole lot of them, including her own, would go somewhere else to play. But not for long. Actually she was glad to have them here where she and Father Branson could keep an eye on them.

One thing that gave her no little cause for concern was the fact that Rickie and Betsy quarreled so much. Rickie was old enough to keep the peace if he wished, but he showed no desire to do so.

"You should be nicer to your little sister, Rickie," Myra protested.

"Somebody has to keep her level. Everybody else spoils her to death."

Which was the truth. Everyone spoiled her—her father, her teacher, the children at school. Maybe Rickie had something.

"Besides," he went on, "she's a show-off. If there's anything in the world I despise it's a loud-mouthed girl. And here I've gone and got one for a sister. And she shouldn't be playing on that bar, either . . ."

He was very adult and wise. Before his reasoning, Myra felt humble and young. Tomorrow, for sure, she'd better find a way to tell Betsy about not playing on the bars—when boys were in the yard, anyway. That would mean giving them up entirely, though, for the yard was full of boys most of the time. What they should do was move to another neighborhood, one where Betsy would have girls to play with. This street ran to boys and Betsy was growing

more tomboyish every day.

Even as she was thinking these things, the door opened and in came her two children.

"Good heavens," Myra cried out, "what's wrong—"

Rickie's nose was bleeding. His face was covered with blood.

"Have you two been *fighting*—"

"Yes, ma'am," Betsy told her. She looked as if she still had plenty of fight left in her.

"They called Betsy names," Rickie explained.

"And we fought 'em," Betsy put in.

Myra looked at her disheveled daughter. The child had probably brought it on herself. Rickie was right—long ago she should have put a stop to that hanging on bars.

"Betsy, you go upstairs and take a bath. I'll be up to help you in a few minutes. And Rickie you go down to the shower in the basement."

In the bathroom Betsy sat, a small island in a tub of foam.

"They called me a loud-mouthed brat," Betsy said, lifting a handful of suds and letting them run down her shoulders. "And then Rickie jumped on 'em—four of 'em, Mummy. And then I jumped in too. Say, Mummy, can I have my pigtails cut off? If it hadn't been for them, Rick and I could have whipped those boys. They got hold of my pigtails and Rickie had to let go his boy so he could help me out—"

Myra turned suddenly toward the door. There was no changing Betsy.

Father Branson died the following spring. It did not seem possible that the passing of such a quiet and gentle person could leave so great a gap in a family circle. The house seemed empty and lost without him.

He left a life-insurance policy larger than anyone knew he had carried. Because of this, they began to talk house again. Hill and Branson was over the hump, and doing well. It seemed like a good time to build.

By this time they had both given up the idea of a Spanish-type house. A Cape Cod Colonial seemed to fit better into their needs. They bought a lot in the Mill Creek addition. Although it was new, there was a good school with nice children for Rickie and Betsy to have for friends. Dick brought home the plans and spread them out on the dining-room table. He and Myra worked together on them, with the children coming by to offer suggestions frequently.

Myra sat at the dining-room table one afternoon, looking over the plans. It was Saturday and the yard was full of boys, as usual. Betsy, graduated at last from the bars, was standing up in the swing, pushing it higher and higher with every sweep.

"Watch me," she was yelling.

Myra sighed, thinking of how much the child still had to learn. Just then Dick came in.

"Hello, darling," she said. "Just looking over the plans—"

"Happy?" he asked.

"Oh, yes," she said.

He didn't mean about the house and they both knew it.

She stood up and he came to her, put his arms around her. She dropped her arms around his neck in a gesture almost as automatic as the one she had used, years ago, the time he had first kissed her. Standing so, they seemed to achieve a completeness, as if only when they were together did either one become the real person he was meant to be.

It was then that they heard the screams in the yard, the awful sickening thud.

They ran together, she and Dick, through the kitchen, across the porch, out to the back yard. The boys were all huddled together in a tight circle of horror and excitement. The core of that circle was Betsy. Myra pushed her way through to her, saw the little body flattened out against the flagstones as if it had been beaten down into them.

"She—she just seemed to *shoot* out of the swing," one of the boys said.

Dick put a restraining hand on Myra's shoulder. "Don't touch her, Myra," he said. "We can't move her until the doctor comes."

They turned the dining room into a sick-room for Betsy.

The New House

They did not take her to the hospital because her life hung by so slender a thread that the slightest unnecessary movement might snap it. Someone rolled up the house plans and put them away; outside of that, and the addition of hospital equipment, the room changed very little.

It was a long hard time. There were days when nobody but Myra and Dick gave Betsy even a fighting chance. Then there was the day when the doctor said yes, she'd live—but she would always be a cripple. There were two operations. There was the day when she took a few halting steps, with Dick on one side to support her and Myra on the other.

It was weeks later when she walked by herself to the sunny bay window where her dolls sat. That was a victory and a triumph.

"It will take time," the doctor said. "She is still afraid. She will do better as she becomes more confident."

He meant, of course, that she would not limp so much.

There were the endless exercises, the massaging. And finally, the corrective shoe which must be fitted expertly, watched carefully.

Then one warm day she limped out into the yard to watch Rickie shoot goals. But she kept her face averted from the swing still hanging from the elm tree and the look on her face was hard for Myra to bear. Each day she went out now. Rickie did not pay any attention to her—just let her watch. And then one day Myra heard her say, "Rickie, put me in the swing. I want to swing."

Myra stood perfectly still. So much depended on this moment—so much—

"Oh, gosh," Rickie said. Just the right touch of older-brother disgust, making it seem a casual thing she asked.

He followed her to the swing; he helped her into it. He held her just a moment and then he swung her gently forward. Betsy's face was white and tense. Rickie swung her a little higher. Then suddenly fear dissolved from her face. She laughed.

"Higher," she cried. "*Swing me higher!*"

Myra sat down suddenly on the couch and began to cry.

The months went by. The exercises and the massaging continued. Betsy was in junior high school. Twice now the corrective shoe had been changed; each time the correction was slightly less. Betsy limped only a little. Really, the child had come through admirably. She spent most of her time playing in the yard; the boys endured her, even encouraged her. They found new ways for her to exercise and were proud of her progress. Where once Betsy had been a wild little hoyden, now she had an anchored gladness, a disciplined joy. . . .

They began to plan the house again. This time it was for sure. It was to be ranch style. Although they did not say so, they knew they chose this because of Betsy. Stairs would not be easy for her for years to come. They kept the plans on the dining-room table and the entire family hung over them, each wanting to contribute his own suggestion. Myra was a little disturbed to see how few things they were all agreed upon. Dick was going to have a hard time incorporating all their ideas into a house that would look as if an architect had built it.

They pushed aside the plans one evening to go to the high school basketball game. Rickie had made the team. He was a good player—not spectacular, but dependable. Myra found herself wishing Father Branson could see him tonight. He was snatching the ball off the boards, darting in and out among the opponents, playing a good steady game. But even so, things were going against the home team. With only seconds to play, they were one point behind. And then Rickie had the ball. He was flashing down the length of the court, dribbling the ball ahead of him. As he neared the goal, the watchers stood up on the bleachers, yelling his name. Rickie Branson's name! To the heady tune of it he sank the ball through the basket, just a split second before the whistle blew.

Myra stood with them, remembering the serious little boy shooting goals through endless afternoons. She felt Dick reach for her hand, knew he was remembering too. Betsy was jumping up and down, yelling herself hoarse, sparing the injured leg not at all.

After the game they sat around the dining-room table, drinking cocoa, talking things over. Rickie had sprawled out on the couch, completely exhausted.

"Oh, Rick," Betsy trilled, "you were wonderful, *wonderful.*"

"Oh, cut it," Rickie said. But he was pleased. He looked over at the table, where the plans lay.

"I want a basket on the back of the house," he said.

"Couldn't we have it in the yard?" Myra asked.

"I guess so. But I got used to practicing on one against the house and I wouldn't know how to gauge my shots—"

"And I want a bay window in the dining room," Betsy said, looking at this one where her schoolbooks lay, with her red scarf on top of them.

Dick squinted at the plans. "I think we ought to have a workshop in the basement," he said. "And a shower."

"We ought to go to bed," Myra said idly. As she spoke she was thinking of how much she'd miss upstairs bedrooms. When you got in a hurry, you could shut them off and forget them.

"I want a swing in the back yard," Betsy said. "Just like this one here—"

Myra looked up quickly to protest. Betsy was getting too big for a swing. That would have to go.

And then the strangest thing happened.

It was as if she saw this house—the one they lived in now

—for the first time, with that same feeling of rightness and completeness she had known, years ago, that day when she first discovered the miracle of Dick's love. All the multiple threads of the days which had woven themselves into this house, into their lives, flashed before her. Dick, looking up from the page he was reading aloud. Betsy, making paper dolls. Rickie trying to catch the sunbeam on the couch. In the house was caught all the distilled essence of the things that had happened to them. Living here, they had become what they were. So much were they and this house interwoven that now the only sure thing they knew about the new house was that they wanted it to be like this one.

Which was not strange. For this was not just a house—it was the texture of their lives, the home of all their hearts.

She stood up. She began to roll up the plans.

"Dick—" she said.

Wasn't it wonderful! Even before she spoke, he knew what she was going to say. Knew it, because it was what he wanted her to say.

The Boy in the Back Seat

HE WAS THE BOY NOBODY EVER NOTICED PARTICULARLY. HIS features had the look of not being quite assembled yet. By and by when time had set its stamp, his face might turn out to be strong and interesting—provided the right things happened to him in the interim. But now he was eighteen and faded into the background.

She was the girl who reminded people of a scarlet tanager in flight, or a crimson maple leaf blowing through October. There was a gaiety about her, a careless sweetness. She was a child stretching its hands toward a sunbeam, a child with hair soft and reddish brown, and eyes of light-flecked hazel.

Oh, she was lovely all right, and everyone knew her and called her by name. "Hi, Marcia," they would say, the sound of the greeting making a warm and friendly sound which followed her down the hall. "Good morning, Marcia," teachers would say inside the classrooms. There was warmth in their voices, too, although she was only a middling-good student.

His name was Bill Handley, but sometimes the teachers fumbled it. That was because he always sat on the back seat and seldom volunteered an answer. When the teachers checked his written work, they were surprised. Once the science teacher made him take a test over; his grade was so high she thought he had cheated. He made an even higher grade.

"His paper was better than Nelda Thorpe's." (She was the earnest one, the worker. Mostly teachers gave her A's without bothering to read her papers through.) "He's smart, I guess. Just lazy."

"No," Miss Courtney told her. (Miss Courtney was the history teacher, the shy, retiring, left-out one.) "That's not it at all—"

She wished she could find words to make them see that Bill's difficulty lay in the fact that he could walk home with all the honors there were in school and there'd be no one to tell about them. For the people Bill Handley stayed with made no bones of the fact that they had adopted him when he was ten so he could help around the dairy they ran. They thought they were doing well by him when they let him go to high school at all. They weren't bad people —just dull and stupid and with little warmth about them.

But Miss Courtney didn't say these things. She tried, but gave up because people mostly didn't listen to her either.

The Boy in the Back Seat

So Bill went on his way, not talking much to anyone except Miss Courtney, and little enough to her. He didn't come to games and that sort of thing, because he had to go right home after school. By the time he got to class in the morning, he had already been up for hours, and was glad just to sit quietly in his back seat.

"Dreaming," the science teacher said. She was still a little nettled over her mistake.

This time she was right, however; Bill *was* dreaming. He was dreaming of Marcia McCauley.

For she was all the loveliness of his world—scent of apple blossoms after rain, call of a field lark in early spring, crisp tang of apples stored against winter's need. He would try her name over to himself sometimes as he sat with his head buried in the flank of a cow. "Marcia McCauley," he would whisper softly, feeling no incongruity about bringing the poetry of her name into the barn. She was a part of his consciousness; her name his to say. "Marcia—Marcia Mc-Cauley."

His boldness left him when he met her in the school halls. He ventured a "Hello" without adding her name. She would answer "Hi" without adding his name either. But that was because she simply did not know his name.

And then a wonderful and unbelievable thing happened. She was transferred into Miss Courtney's history class, the one Bill was in. The class had been in session several weeks, so things were pretty well jolted down. There were only two vacant seats left—one in the front row, next to the conscientious Nelda, and the other in the back row next to Bill.

"Take your choice," Miss Courtney said.

Marcia never even hesitated. She worked her way past Nelda, back to the seat next to Bill.

"Hi," she said, settling herself into it. "I'm Marcia Mc-Cauley."

He wanted to tell her he knew that, but all he said was, "I'm Bill Handley."

"I bet you people are so far ahead I'll never catch up."

"We haven't done so much," he assured her. "You can have my notes if you want them."

"Oh, thank you," she said warmly.

She made it sound as though he had done something generous and fine.

"I'm no good in history," she confided. "Mostly it's dates, and I can't remember them. They don't seem important. I mean, what difference does it make *when* a thing happened? All we need to know is that it *did* happen."

"Yeah," Bill agreed.

But all the time he was thinking that some dates were important. He'd never forget this one: Monday, October 16.

The next morning Bill took a great deal of pains with himself before starting to school. He washed his hands and cleaned his nails. He combed his hair carefully. And though it was only Tuesday, and the rule was he got a fresh shirt on Mondays and Wednesdays, he put on a clean one anyway. When Mrs. Dingley, the woman he lived with, protested, he told her he was mixed up in the days. But he didn't take off the shirt. He wore his best sweater, too—the one he was supposed to keep for special occasions.

When he met Marcia in the hall before class he said, "Hi, Marcia." It sounded fine, the way it slipped off his tongue. She answered "Hi," giving him a bright inclusive glance that held no real sign of recognition. And suddenly he felt that maybe he *had* been foolish to wear the clean shirt. He went into the classroom.

Nelda Thorpe was already in her seat, making a few careful notes on her paper.

"Hello, Bill," she said. She looked as if she would say more if he encouraged her, but he worked his way on back to his own place, sat down and opened his book. Then he heard a voice beside him.

"Why, Bill," Marcia said, dropping a few books and a couple of papers before she finally got seated. "How nice you look."

Delight washed through him, spilling over into his face. He bent to pick up the books and papers, and when he handed them to Marcia, he was conscious of the fact that Miss Courtney had come into the room and was watching him with a thoughtful expression on her vague little face. He saw her take up a pencil and make a note or two on some papers on her desk, and then she called the class to order.

"I'm appointing some committees to work on this new unit we're taking up on England," she said. (All the students laughed at Miss Courtney and her committees. They said if sixteen lions rushed into the room at the same time, she wouldn't let a pupil budge until a committee in charge of exit had been appointed.) She went on now, droning out the lists—one for religion, one for public works, one for the money system.

"The committee on law," she said, "will consist of Marcia McCauley, Bill Handley—"

Bill didn't listen past his name. He was wondering how he could manage to stay for the meeting, which was scheduled for four o'clock, and still get home in time to do the chores. Marcia, chairman by virtue of the fact that her name had been called first, solved the problem.

"I can't meet at four this afternoon," she said. "Why don't you all come to my house this evening, say about seven-thirty?"

"I'll make it," Bill said, resolution in his voice. "I may be a little late, but I'll be there."

Bill walked up on the McCauley front porch. He was late, as he knew he would be, but he was there, as he had promised. He hoped Marcia herself would answer his knock —he felt a shyness about meeting her father, who was a banker and quite an important man around town. What would he say if Mr. McCauley came? At that moment, Marcia opened the door.

"Hi, Bill," she said. "I'm sure glad you came."

The McCauley house had a fireplace in the living room and some dark and solid furniture and rugs that were a little faded but were soft underfoot and lovely to look at anyway. There were books in shelves around the wall, and fragile vases and things on tables and whatnots. Soft satiny stuff hung at the windows. Bill had never seen a room like this. He would have liked to stand there and look for a while.

"Come on," Marcia said. "We're working back in the playroom. Only we haven't done a single thing yet. I guess we were waiting for you."

She giggled a little when she said it, and suddenly Bill felt at home, and necessary.

Ushering Bill in, she said, "You all know Bill."

Yes, they all knew him, and their welcome was sweet. Bill took the chair Marcia indicated, the one next to Chuck Horgan. Chuck was the most popular boy in school. He played football and then, when the season was over, turned to basketball. He had money and a car of his own and everyone liked him. Every once in a while it occurred to Bill to wonder how it would feel to be Chuck Horgan.

"You know anything about English laws, Bill?" Chuck asked. "If you do, you better get us going on something, and quick."

"Well," Bill said, clearing his throat, "aren't our laws sort of based on them? Why don't we go ask some lawyer about it?"

"Why, Bill," Marcia said, honest respect in her eyes, "of course. That's the thing to do. We could ask Judge Fielding, only I can't go with the group. He's my godfather and he still thinks I'm six months old. He'd only joke with us if I went. Why don't you go, Bill? The rest of us could read things in books."

"Who, me?" Bill asked in amazement.

"Sure, you. You're the one who thought of it."

Everyone on the committee said yes, he was the one to go, and voted on it just to make it right. Then Marcia said the business was finished and she went out to the kitchen and came back with popcorn and apples and cookies and milk. Chuck pulled out the tennis table from the corner and they began to play. Someone pushed a paddle into Bill's hand. He had never played before, but they all said he did fine.

Several times, in the days that followed, Bill almost backed out on going to see Judge Fielding. Who was he,

The Boy in the Back Seat

Bill Handley, to take up the time of a busy man, an important man? He was crazy to have agreed to go in the first place.

And then he remembered how sure Marcia had been that he would do it, and he knew he could not disappoint her. So he called the judge himself, feeling his voice getting stiff and unnatural as he asked for the appointment. The man said to be sure—to come Saturday afternoon at two.

Promptly at two on Saturday afternoon, Bill, wearing his best clothes, walked into the judge's office. The man was very cordial. He talked to Bill straight and honest— good man-to-man talk. He started off with English law and then got around to law in general, and Bill began to see the beauty and order of law. It made sense. There were a rightness and a precision about it, a justice and a strength. A person could depend on law. He was thinking it was a fine thing to be a lawyer, a good and honorable thing. It was as if the judge read the boy's mind.

"Ever think of being a lawyer yourself?" he asked.

"Well, no," the boy said slowly.

"You'd make a good one," Judge Fielding told him.

"Thank you, sir," Bill said, standing up to leave.

"Oh, that's all right. If I can ever be of any more help to you, be sure to call on me."

The judge extended his hand. The interview was over.

217

Actually, Bill had thought it wouldn't take him more than five minutes—ten, at the most—to give his report. When he stood up he had a strange fluttery feeling in his stomach and the faces of his classmates blurred a little, so that they were all of a piece. Then they began to focus and he could distinguish the individual features. He saw Nelda Thorpe, her face intent and quiet, leaning a little forward in her chair. He looked beyond her and saw Marcia, and suddenly he began to talk, and it was to her, and no one else, he sent his words. He was trying to tell her all the things Judge Fielding had said about the law—how the whole universe was built around it. And even as he talked, the great dream was born. *Someday he was going to be a lawyer.* The spell of the dream loosed his tongue and he talked on and on. The next thing he knew, the bell was ringing.

It was Nelda Thorpe who led the applause—and that was pretty fine, because mostly the class was just relieved when a report was finished. Bill worked his way back to his seat, and the sound of his mates' approval was sweet to his ear.

"Oh, Bill," Marcia said as he sat down, "you were *wonderful*—just *real* wonderful. All along I knew you could do it."

Bill was too wise to think that one good report would make school over for him. He continued to get A's in history, but for the most part he still sat in the rest of his classes, letting the other, more pushing students do the talking. More people noticed him in the halls, and he liked that. And Marcia spoke first now.

"Hi, Bill," she'd say. "See you in a minute."

And off she'd go down the hall, stopping to talk with everyone—not just the popular ones. Almost the whole class would be seated before Marcia finally came in. She would slide past them, apologizing, "Oh, I'm sorry—did I step on you—oh, excuse me, please!"

Because it was Marcia, they smiled.

Even Miss Courtney was not cross with her when she did not have her lessons. Sometimes she forgot assignments or left papers at home. Once she left her books in Chuck Horgan's jalopy and the next morning he came down with measles. It was a week before she remembered where the books were and then she had to have another set issued to her. Everyone thought it was a good joke.

"I'll bet it was all put on, your forgetting," they quipped. "Where else would they be?"

But the way Bill saw it, she never forgot the really important things—like being thoughtful of people. And generous. He liked to watch her talking and laughing. He liked the way she looked—her hair shining, curling up a little in the back, glinting when the sun shone on it; and so clean —as if she took a bath every single morning and put on fresh clothes from the skin out. She always smelled sweet; it wasn't quite the perfume she used—it was just a good clean smell. Bill could tell when she came close to him, even if he didn't see her.

The year slipped into spring. It was a magic time, with gentle rains, then sunshine, and flowers blooming earlier than usual, making the whole world a wash of sweetness. Everyone said there had never been such a spring before, and Bill knew it was so. Everything had a glow and he a sureness. The things he did, both at home and at school, seemed to turn out well. He finished his chores easily, and quickly, managing always to be in his seat at school early. Some morning Marcia would come early—it was bound to happen because things were all working out right for him this spring. Then he would have a chance to tell her about being a lawyer.

But the days slipped by and she did not come. Always Nelda was there, bending over her books, and she would look up and say, "Hello, Bill." And he would answer, "Hi," and go to work at once. Wasn't it funny? He thought briefly —Nelda was pretty, sort of. Feature by feature, she was probably as pretty as Marcia. But she wasn't Marcia—there was no glow to her, no gaiety. She was just another girl. Marcia was . . . Marcia.

And then one morning it happened, just as he knew it must happen if he were only patient. Marcia rushed in a good ten minutes before time for class.

"Hi, Bill," she said. "I have to get these lists copied before class starts. They're the committees for the May Day dance."

"Give me some," Bill said. "I'll help."

"Oh, Bill—that's a dear—"

He took the lists, began copying them. There she was, right at his side. And yet he couldn't tell her, with her rushing like mad to finish her share of the lists and Nelda Thorpe sitting up there in her seat, within easy earshot. If he just could be with her alone for a while. He passed his lists to her and then he heard himself saying words he never thought he'd speak.

"Marcia," he was saying, "I was wondering—could I take you to the May Day dance—"

"Why, Bill," Marcia said, "that is such a sweet thing for you to do."

She looked at him with a great warmth and gratitude. Just then the bell rang and Miss Courtney called the class to order. Bill scarcely heard her. How natural and wonderfull it had all turned out. He would take Marcia to the May Day dance, and then he'd have time enough to tell her how he was going to be a lawyer.

Bill stood at the McCauley door. In his hands was a florist box. He had on his best suit and he had taken a great deal of pains with himself. Even Mrs. Dingley had been impressed.

"You look real nice," she had said. "I guess you'll be home late." Something seemed to move her—a kindness, a belated stirring. "You go on and sleep in the morning. I'll help with the milking."

"Oh, no," Bill had said. "Thanks a lot, but I'll do it." He'd feel all right in the morning—he'd feel wonderful.

He knocked at the door, and Marcia herself answered. She had on a dress that looked like a cloud, only clouds were never blue like this. The neck was low and there were no sleeves at all. Her skin showed, very fine-grained and lovely.

"Why, Bill," she said, looking at him blankly. "Won't you . . . come in?"

He followed her into the living room, still holding his box of flowers. A little chill ran over him. Didn't she think he looked right, or something? Or did she think they'd have to go on the bus, since he hadn't come for her in a car? Actually, he had thought the bus would be all right, but now he could see she couldn't ride the bus, wearing that dress. He had a couple dollars left; he'd call a taxi. He'd never ridden in one and he might not know just how to go about it, but he'd manage that. He held out the box.

"Here are some flowers for you," he said. "The man

said white would go with anything."

She took the box. She was trying to act like herself, but she couldn't. Something was dead sure wrong.

"What's the matter, Marcia?" he asked awkwardly. "I mean, are you sick or something? We don't have to go if you are."

She stood twisting the string on the box of flowers. She looked at him nervously.

"Bill," she began, "did you—I mean, well, did you think you had a date with me tonight?"

Did he think he had a date with her! He had asked her, and she hadn't said no. Surely she remembered that.

And then it hit him. He had asked her and she hadn't said no. But she hadn't said yes, either. She hadn't really answered at all. Maybe she hadn't even heard him. Maybe she was talking about its being sweet for him to copy the lists! He had thought—oh, fool that he was, he had thought that her words, which were nothing more than the kindness she showed to everyone, meant consent.

And then memory came to her too.

"Oh, Bill! That day you mentioned it in class . . . Miss Courtney stopped us before I had time to answer. Bill, I couldn't have said yes, even then. I've had a date with Chuck for months—long before you asked me."

Watching compassion flood her face, he stood unable to

223

speak, knowing his shame and his misery showed.

Pity, from her! Anger and a vast humiliation engulfed him. Pride rose and he flushed darkly, and then went very white.

"Oh, that's all right," he told her, his voice sounding harsh and stiff in his own ears. He turned, started toward the door. "Forget about it."

"Bill!" she cried. "Listen—you come with Chuck and me. I'll give you my program and you can put down as many dances as you want. We—we'd like you to go with us. I'll call Chuck. He'll understand—"

She made a motion toward the phone, her eyes wide and unhappy. Upset as he was, Bill remembered she couldn't bear to hurt people.

"No," he said. "No." Not her pity. His voice sounded like thunder in his ears. "*No!*"

His hand stopped her. He took her by the arm and pulled her around until she faced him. She was close to him— closer than she had ever been before, even in dreams. And how it happened he did not know, but she was in his arms. Sweetness and beauty and exaltation—oh, more than anything, that—swept over him in waves, and he bent and kissed her full upon the lips.

For just a moment he felt them quiver under his. It was he who drew away first. He turned and walked out into the night.

Bill went across the fields, back to the farm. He walked very fast, as if, by so doing, he could outrun the truth. But the truth ran at his side; it ran ahead and lay in wait for him. It shouted to him that he had been a fool.

All year he had lived in a dream, a dream that Marcia really cared what happened to him; whether he came to class or stayed away; whether he did well or poorly; whether he became a lawyer or spent the rest of his life with his head on a cow's flank. All the time she had cared no more for him than she did for all the others—those shabby, left-out ones she smiled at when she met them in the halls.

Even now she was, in all likelihood, laughing at him—she and Chuck Horgan and her happy crowd. "I was never so embarrassed in my life," she would be saying. And the others would ask, "What did you *do*, Marcia?" And she would say, "I asked him to come with us, of course."

All along she had felt nothing for him but pity. He strove to make the hurt and humiliation of that burn out the last vestige of his dream. But thoughts of Marcia kept coming: the way she looked in the blue dress; the warmth in her voice when she urged him to go with her and Chuck. She wasn't laughing then. And she wasn't laughing when he kissed her.

Her lips had been warm and soft. They had trembled a little under his, as if ready to respond. He let himself re-member what it felt like to hold her in his arms, and slowly the bitterness died a little, and the hurt. Not entirely, but some of it. He walked more slowly, and he unclenched his hands at his sides. He lifted his eyes, and saw the sky, all shot with stars. One, the brightest of the lot, might have been Marcia—far away, yet bright and lovely. And friendly. He stopped, head raised. It was a long look, and when he had finished he felt quieter. And older, someway; wiser.

"She'll never pity me again," he said finally, speaking aloud. "I'll show her. I don't know how, yet, but I will. Someday I'll come back here and all of them—every one of them—will be proud of me. I'll show them."

It was twenty years before he came back and by that time he had forgotten his vow. He came because his class had asked him to speak at the reunion, as their most famous member. He was a big man in the state. There was even talk of running him for governor. People needed to be reminded that he started out a poor boy, worked his way through law school, and all that. Of course, a woman like his wife was a great asset to any man, politician or what have you.

He walked down the halls of the high school that day of home-coming—a big man, not handsome especially, but distinguished-looking, with a strong intelligent face, a confident sureness about him. A good man—one to be trusted.

"Hi, Bill," everyone said, crowding around him. "Hi,

Bill, remember me?"

Their greetings made a pleasant sound, following him down the corridors.

The wife at his side was a lovely woman with a look of happiness that carried over to other people. A little absent-minded, perhaps, as any woman would be with three school-age children left at home.

Miss Courtney came across the room to meet them, her glasses slipping down on her little button nose.

"Remember me, Bill?" she asked. It was a big thing to her that he should remember. "I'm so proud of you."

"Sure," Bill said. "My, it's good to see you. You're Miss Courtney. You remember my wife, don't you?"

"I . . ." They could see her trying, mentally running down the hundreds of class rolls she had taken through the years.

Bill's wife put out her hand. "There were so many of us, you couldn't possibly remember," she said, smiling warmly. "I was Marcia McCauley."

"Oh, of course," Miss Courtney said, still flustered.

"It's no wonder you forgot me," Marcia Handley went on. "As soon as I graduated"—she paused a moment—"I followed Bill down to State."

Between husband and wife something flew: a memory, never to be forgotten; a joy, never to be outlived; a knowl-edge that the thing which she had just said constituted the

227

great explanation of their lives. That even now, neither of them could say those simple words without having the beauty and the wonder return.

"I would have remembered you, all right," Miss Courtney went on, trying to justify her lapse of memory, "if only I had looked at you. But for the moment, I couldn't see anyone but Bill."

Marcia said, "I'm used to that. Nobody ever notices me when Bill's around."

But the way she said it, anyone could tell she didn't mind a bit. That, if it were really true, it was probably her own doings that made it so, and that things were quite the way she would have them.

Bonus of Happiness

WHEN PROFESSOR PAUL ELROD CUT ACROSS THE CAMPUS MONday morning on his way to his office in Macy Hall, he noticed that Saturday night's light frost had turned the ash tree by the fountain to a splash of gold. He was glad to see it. In some indefinable way this tree, which was always the first to turn, signaled the real beginning of school, regardless of what the catalogues had to say. By this time the girls, who had brought only fall clothes, were finding sweaters and skirts more comfortable. The football boys had ceased to be entirely depleted by the rigors of fall practice. And those who had known the cruel hurt of rush week had progressed into sensible acceptance, or at least into silent endurance.

By now, too, the Professor himself was beginning to know his students well enough to be able to distinguish those who wanted to learn from those who were merely there; those whose problems were of a fleeting nature from the ones with difficulties deeper and more subtle. It was in this latter group that young Bill Gregory belonged—Bill Gregory, who always came alone to class, ahead of the others, so that he could finish without witnesses the clumsy business of settling himself, and his cane and his leg, into the chair at the back of the classroom.

Professor Elrod had not yet settled in his own mind the correct way to deal with the boy and his problem. Bill Gregory, back after nearly two years to enroll once more as a freshman. Sitting, almost unnoticed, among the newcomers who knew only vaguely, if at all, about that other Bill Gregory, the one who had come to Barstow on a football scholarship and been elected, almost immediately, captain of the freshman football team, president of the freshman class, and most popular freshman on the campus. Even so, Professor Elrod remembered him as having been a highly promising student.

Instead, here was this new Bill Gregory, the one who had been struck down by polio in the middle of his first semester, his right arm now hanging useless at his side, his right leg held rigid in a brace, and on his face a look of bleak emptiness, an expression somewhere between a man's hurt and a child's disillusionment.

Professor Elrod let himself into his office now, sat down at his desk, and began idly to sort papers. From the stack he drew Bill's, looked at it intently, as if he hoped that by so doing he might glean the answer to the boy's problem. But even as he did so, he knew the effort was futile; the boy's paper was correct, even formal, but in it there was no hint of his own inner conflict. Actually, he did not need to be taking this class at all, for already he had learned all about emphasis and coherence and the rest of the things freshman composition was supposed to teach him.

But the boy had not yet learned to manage either the cane or his need for it. Still, he did not seem to mind the cane so much as he did the thing it represented—the fact that his young body was an imperfect thing and must forever remain so. And even that was not the worst of it: the empty look appeared to haunt his face because he felt that his own imperfection came out of an imperfect world which must, too, forever remain so. His sadness was for the world and not for himself, save as his own condition mirrored the world's sad state.

Lois Elrod, the Professor's wife, always had the same suggestion for helping any student in difficulties—she was all for giving him a good book to read. But the Professor himself knew this case would not be solved so easily, for the boy, if anything, retreated too much into the world of books. Professor Elrod was sure of these things, even as he was sure that he could not ignore the problem of that empty face. It was a knowledge that had come to him from far away and long ago—something he did not consciously think about too much these days.

Yet it was something he thought about all the time, something that underlay all his thought, as a house is undergirded by the strong framework that must forever remain unseen.

Professor Elrod's mind went slipping back across the years to the time when he himself, neither Doctor nor Professor then, was in Barstow University, working on his doctorate. He was there both because the school was one of the best in his field—English—and because he could get a teaching fellowship which would help pay his expenses. No, that was not quite the way of it. He was there because Lois had willed it so. The will of Lois was a mighty thing. It had discovered him while they were both in college, he a freshman, she a senior and had decided that teaching was the job for him. It was she, too, who after their marriage planned that he must work toward a position in college.

"That's the place for men teachers," she told him. "You'll get your Master's, and then your Doctor's, and teach in college."

(It had come out as she said. In the retelling, it sounded so simple, like a statement about the Creation from the book of Genesis. He was Dr. Paul Elrod now, and teaching in college.)

But then he had only started on the Doctor's, and was liking no part of it. He resented the fact that, even with the help of the fellowship, he did not make enough money to provide for himself and Lois, so she stayed home and taught to help finance the venture. He did not like the way his classes sat, eyeing him with indifference or, at best, with polite endurance. He did not like the daily mountains of papers which must be checked. More than any of these, he disliked the fact that he was committed to teaching now, with no turning back.

The great burden of his discontent was spilling over him one morning when a new student walked into the class.

"Hello," she said, smiling a little as she laid her enrollment slip on his desk. "I hope I'm not too late to get in."

For a week now he had been looking at freshmen girls all so curiously alike that he might well have been viewing one of them in a multiple mirror. This girl was different. For one thing, she must be older than the rest—twenty-two or twenty-three, perhaps. Her hair was long, worn in a knot at the back of her neck. It had a bronze cast to it; now, in the light, it seemed ready to burst into flame. Later he was to know that, in shadow, it dimmed to a light brown. She wore very little make-up, and her skin had a clear translucence. Her eyes regarded him with a look at once childlike and mature.

"I'm Amy Wingate," she told him. "I'm sorry to be late, but I'll make up the work."

Paul Elrod, a good ten years older than she, felt curiously, inarticulately young. He glanced down at her papers, found them all in order.

"Oh, that's all right," he found himself saying a little

stiffly. "If you'll come to my office this afternoon about four, I'll give you the back assignments."

She was at his office promptly at four. He sat at a desk piled high with papers, and he must have been regarding them with a look of helpless distaste, for scarcely was she finished getting the list of make-up work, when she turned to him to say impulsively:

"Listen—why don't you let me help you with the grading? I'd like to, really."

"Why, I—" Paul hesitated. He didn't have the money to pay her. But before he could finish, she went on.

"It would be a real favor if you'd let me," she told him. "I've been helping my father with his books and articles, and now that he's—he's gone, I need something to do to take up my time."

"Well—" Paul began.

"I mean it," she said earnestly.

He knew she did mean it—that giving her the work would be a real favor. He understood now why she was different from the others, why she was older.

"You'll never know how much this is going to help me," he told her. "Pick up as many as you think you can stand and bring them back when you've finished with them."

"Oh, thank you," she said.

And so, it started.

Bonus of Happiness

The fall was golden and lovely, with the air so still that a leaf hung suspended a long time before it fell. The sky had a bright expectancy about it, as if summer, not winter, lay ahead. Each day had a feeling of beauty poised as lightly as a moth. Time held a fused quality; yesterday merged into today, and today was only the first part of tomorrow. It seemed almost wrong to waste such days sitting inside making red marks on freshman themes. Paul said as much to Amy one Saturday afternoon when she walked in to leave some papers and pick up others.

"Let's chuck them and go for a walk," he suggested.

"Why not?" she agreed.

They cut across the campus, stopping at the Co-op long enough for Paul to buy apples and milk chocolates, and then took the path that led down to the lake. Neither one had much to say, but both felt a sense of adventure and daring in their exploit. They were two children playing an innocent game of hooky. Presently they came to a spot where the trees opened up to form a small flat amphitheater at the lake's edge. By common agreement they sat down, and Paul took the chocolates and apples out of his pockets.

"Strange sort of weather," he said, munching. "Seems to be saying that this thing which can't last is really going to last forever."

"Lots of things do that," she remarked.

"For instance?"

"Railroad stations, for one thing. And highways. And colleges."

"Colleges?" He shifted his position so quietly that a red squirrel watching him did not feel called upon to move at all. "Colleges and railroad stations. Funny comparison. What made you think of that?"

"People are just there for a little while," she explained, "while they wait to go on somewhere else."

"That's time itself," he said. "A day is just something we go through on our way to another one."

She looked at him strangely. "I'd better be getting back," she said.

She got to her feet, lightly as a spring uncoiling. He joined her, and they started back to the campus, leaving the lake glinting bluely in the sun.

"See you Monday?"

"Yes—Monday—"

The golden weather lasted. Amy thought it would be fun to cook their supper out, so they took wieners and buns and a thermos jug of coffee down by the lake. Paul made a small fire, sharpened sticks for roasting the wieners.

"You're quite a woodsman," Amy said, watching him. "You ought to be tramping the woods somewhere with a gun on your shoulder and then go home at night to write essays, like Thoreau."

When he reminded her that Thoreau would never have carried a gun, she said, oh, bother, she wouldn't want him to be like Thoreau, anyway. He was too coldly intellectual. And when he asked her what she did want him to be like, she said:

"Like yourself—a nice kindly professor who looks like Gary Cooper. Ten years from now you'll be a little gray around the temples, and the college will be using your pictures in the catalogue, for bait."

(Well, she had been right. Every time he saw one of those pictures he thought of Amy. Every time he looked at the gray that framed his face he thought of her.)

"Oh," he said flatly.

"Don't talk like that."

"Like what?"

"As if you found the prospect unendurable. College professors are terribly important. Sort of like the monks who preserved learning in the Middle Ages."

He took her hand and bent the fingers back one at a time. They had a curious springlike quality, bending easily without giving any feeling of weakness. She made no movement to withdraw her hand. The moment was right and perfect, like the weather.

"I'm no monk," he told her.

"No, thank heavens," she agreed.

"Besides," he went on after a while, "I don't even believe I'm going to be much of a teacher. I don't want to be, really."

She sat up straight, turning to face him.

"Oh, but you must," she urged. "I mean, you must want to be a teacher. A college teacher. It's really very important."

"To you, maybe," he conceded. "And maybe to me, more than I realize. But to them—the ones who come to college —it actually matters very little. Class is just something to sit through, and the library a place to meet their dates."

He knew he sounded petulant and complaining, like an old woman fussing because her family neglected her.

"But it *is* important to them," she assured him earnestly. "They may not all show it, but it means something to all of them, even the slow ones. Maybe to them, most of all."

"And may I ask you how?" he said, with that strange feeling he'd had so many times when they were together like this—that she was the teacher, he the student. "They go away and never think of college again, unless there happens to be a good football team that year."

"Of course they go away," she agreed. "That's part of it. They marry and they have children. And all the time you're thinking they've forgotten you, they're really remembering. They know they left something here. They may not quite know what it is, but they do know it's here, and they depend on you to guard it. If they sent their children back for it and found you had betrayed their trust, they'd yell fast enough."

"I can't imagine a freshman yelling over lost knowledge," he said lazily.

"The freshmen most of all," she assured him. "It's important to catch them early. The freshmen and the 'different' ones—you must always watch out for them. Sometimes the things you do for them in those first weeks can determine the whole course of their lives."

"You're an idealist," he told her. He took her hand again, held it against his cheek. "And you know what happens to idealists. They have a pretty thin time of it in this world."

"They have a lovely time," she countered. "You ought to know. You're one yourself."

This he did not deny. And suddenly he knew he wanted to be a teacher. That he had always wanted to be a teacher. The difference was that what he had known before was of the head; now, it was of the heart. And that, he realized, was where real teaching started.

She had not moved her hand at all, not even so much as a finger resting against his cheek. But presently she said, "Don't you think we'd better roast the wieners now?"

And soon there was the smell of wood smoke, and of coffee boiling, and the sound of a fire crackling and of light conversation.

From the first, Paul had been dissatisfied with the subject for his dissertation—a dissatisfaction which stemmed partly from the fact that the idea was Lois's, not his. She wanted him to do something on the minor English poets.

"I think it would be very exciting," she said.

For Lois, the word "exciting" was an adjective applied solely to pursuits of the mind.

So, partly because she was so anxious to have him do it, and partly because he had nothing better of his own to suggest, he was now doing research on those little men, the ones who had each spent a lifetime struggling to write—and then had come up with maybe only one poem which was remembered.

"Sort of a waste of time," he grumbled to Amy.

"Yours or theirs?" she asked.

"Both," he grinned.

"They may have spent a lifetime on one poem," she said. "But think of what they left us. It's as if—as if they poured all the meaning of their lives into that single idea. That's what gives it depth and significance."

He could see what she meant: a lifetime of wisdom and hope and hurt channeled into a few hundred words. No wonder they had force and purpose. That single poem was the distillation of years. It was like collecting all the sun's rays into a single beam of light. The force of it was strong enough to set a flame. And suddenly he could see his work *was* exciting.

"Maybe you're right," he told her.

He knew she was right. His research became alive, meaningful. He felt he was looking at the bare souls of these "little men," and now they, too, became as big as life itself, and truth, and the universe.

The days slipped along, each one more unbelievably lovely than its predecessor. His and Amy's relationship, too, hung suspended as if it were also a golden leaf in the still fall air. Things might have gone on so forever had not the rains come.

They started in the night, and by morning the world was a gray and sodden thing. Paul, working at his desk that afternoon, was filled with nervous unrest. Every time he heard a step in the hall he turned quickly, even though he knew it was foolish to expect Amy to come out on a day like this. By five o'clock he could stand it no longer. He gathered up a sheaf of papers, snatched his hat and coat off the rack, let himself out into the rain.

It was as if other feet than his own took him to the house where she stayed, other hands than his rang the bell. He stood on the porch, waiting for someone to answer the summons, thinking that, as much as they had been together, this was the first time he had been to the house where she stayed. Thinking how little he knew about her, really. That her father had been an invalid and a scholar, and she had helped him with his books. That so long as he lived, she had never felt she could leave him, even to go to college. That her only relatives were some distant cousins, one of whom lived in a little town near by. The nearness of this cousin had influenced her in her decision to come to school here at Barstow.

That was really the extent of his knowledge of her. And now that he thought of it, she knew little more about him. They were both castaways of sorts, adrift on a raft of unreality.

While he was thinking, the door opened, and there stood Amy. She regarded him with surprise.

"Oh, hello," she said. And then, "Won't you come in?"

He followed her into the room.

She was wearing a dark-wine housecoat sort of thing which covered her from neck to ankles. Her hair, a dim brown in the shadows, was tied back with a piece of ribbon. And she wore glasses.

"I was reading," she explained. "Mrs. Matson is gone, and I was lonesome."

She took off her glasses, laid them on the table.

"Sit down," she said.

She motioned him toward a chair and went over to sit on the divan. A book was lying there, face down, and she moved it over to make a place for herself. There was a wood fire in the grate. Except for it, and the reading light over the divan, the room lay in shadow.

"Do sit down," she repeated.

He was still standing. It was as if he were seeing her for the first time as a real person—one who lived in a house and wore glasses and lay on a divan to read before an open fire. Before this, she had been a part of the blueness of the lake, the brightness of the leaves. Their relationship had been a thing of nature—childlike, innocent, natural. Now that he saw her among man-made things—houses, and lights, and yes, even glasses—she became, suddenly, a woman. And he was a man. A married man. From the first she had known about Lois, and her name had passed easily, casually, between them. But now things were different. Constraint sat upon them.

"No," he said, "I'll have to be going. I only came to leave these papers."

Amy got up swiftly, came to him. He sensed her resolve —without knowing the reason for his embarrassment, she still felt it was a threat to their relationship.

"Don't go," she begged. "I'll make some coffee."

She laid her hand upon his arm.

The room went spinning around him.

He must have taken her in his arms, for she was there, resting lightly against him, her arms around his neck. The whole thing was so automatic, so reflexive on both their

243

parts, that it was really impossible to tell how it did happen. He only knew for sure that they were in each other's arms and there was a feeling of rightness about it as if all their lives they had been moving toward this single, beautiful moment, even as those old poets had needed a lifetime to prepare them for one poem of crystal, enduring beauty.

"Amy—" he whispered thickly. And again. "Amy—"

She did not come to class next day. He *had not* really expected her to. He *had* expected her. He felt he could not bear to face the class, seeing her empty chair. He went to his office that afternoon and sat watching the rain, now turning to sleet as it fell. Finally he could stand it no longer. He telephoned her. When she answered, he could not speak for a moment. When he did, he scarcely recognized his voice as his own.

"Hello, Paul," she said. "I was just thinking of you."

"Are you—all right?"

"Yes."

"I'd like to see you."

"I was hoping you would. In fact, I was just thinking about calling you to suggest that you come over."

"Be there in a minute."

The moment she let him in, he sensed a difference in her. For one thing, she wore a suit and high-heeled pumps —much more formal attire than he had ever seen her wear before. But the difference was not all in her clothes. It was as if she had come to some sort of resolution—something that made her sure and at ease.

They went together to the living room, sat down. His nervousness increased, so that suddenly he stood up. Almost at the same instant she stood, too.

They met in the middle of the room and the thing he had told himself must not happen again did happen. Once more she was in his arms. He buried his face in her throat, and even with the whirling of his mind he was conscious of the two worlds there against his face—the smooth, cool impersonalness of the suit fabric against one cheek, the warm softness of her throat against the other. For a moment they stood so, and then she put her hand on his shoulder, pushed him back a little.

"Something has happened to us, hasn't it Paul?" she asked softly.

"Yes—I'm afraid it has."

"Afraid?" she repeated. "Is it anything to be afraid of?"

"No," he told her.

"Neither of us tried to bring it about, did we?" And before he could answer, she went on. "And neither of us feels guilty or ashamed, do we?"

"No, not that," he said. "Not that at all."

"Then why," she asked wisely, "can't we take it as a sort of gift? A bonus of happiness. One of those unearned-increment things the economics people are always talking about."

"Why, indeed?" he said. And kissed her.

They stood so a long time. Presently she said, "But we can't go on with this, you know."

Then she disengaged herself and went to sit on the divan. He came to sit beside her.

"I don't see why not!" he said hotly. "I'll ask Lois for a divorce. She's fair, and kind. She wouldn't want to hold me, if she knew."

Amy looked at him intently. "On what grounds?" she asked.

On what grounds indeed! That he respected her and admired her, yet did not love her? That he had never really loved her? That now he never could, because, even if there was no Amy, he knew the thing which would keep him from ever loving Lois was the fact that, for her, all life's answers lay in books?

He dropped his face in his hands, and sat very still. A log snapped in the fire, sending a blaze up the chimney. A dash of sleet beat against the window.

"It isn't just—just Lois," Amy continued, the name now sounding alien on her lips. "It's those others—the ones you'll teach."

"If you think," he burst out, "that a teacher has to be a sort of nursemaid to a bunch of kids whose own morals are nothing short of pagan, you've got things all wrong!"

"I think," she told him quietly, "that a teacher has to be a nursemaid for decency and right. Not only for the sake of his students, but for his own sake."

"Oh, rot!"

"No," she insisted gently, "I'm right, and you know it. We both know that, regardless of how we feel, we can't do anything about this."

"No," he agreed bitterly, "we can't. I'm ten years older than you, and married besides."

It was the first time the word had passed between them. Until now they had ignored it, side-stepping it deftly, as if their very neglect would make the fact of it cease to exist. No, perhaps that was not quite the way of it. Perhaps they had ignored it as they had ignored the knowledge that they were pupil and teacher; because, in that special sort of relationship which had been theirs, neither thing had seemed important.

"I'm just not the one for you," he went on.

"Oh, yes you are," she told him in a quick rush of eagerness. "I'll never feel toward anyone—" she hesitated, then went on frankly, as if the time for evasion was past. "I'll never love anyone the way I do you."

"You just think that," he told her. "You're young. You were attracted to me because we happened to like the same things, and were lonely, and were thrown together. That's all."

"Do you really believe that?"

"No," he told her honestly. "I don't believe I do."

She was silent again.

"Maybe," he went on, choosing his words carefully, "what I meant was that you'd get over this. Not right away, perhaps, but in time. Then you'll marry someone your own age, and if you think of me at all, it will only be to wonder what you ever saw in me."

She looked at him—a long, slow knowledgeable look.

"Maybe," she said. "It's hard to tell. If I do, though, I know it will be the way a widow marries—not expecting too much. I'll know this is—was—the real thing. Something to cherish, but not to be repeated. Like going to college. Something to hold in my heart, against the years to come."

"Oh, hush," he broke in roughly. "You're talking nonsense."

She reached out, stroked his cheek softly.

"You're so awfully young," she told him, laughing a little. "So much younger than any of your students."

"Listen," he said, a sort of desperate hope urging him on. "Don't decide now. Think it over. Promise me you'll think it over. This is all—well, too sudden for us to know what to do."

She sat still, considering his words.

"Promise me," he repeated. "Promise you'll think about it."

"All right," she finally agreed, "but I don't believe I'll ever see things any differently. I don't believe," she added quietly, "that you really think I should."

He burst into hot denial, but she quieted him.

"I'll go to Cousin Cora's, though, to do my thinking," she told him.

"When will you know?" he asked her.

"I believe I know now," she said. "But I'll think some more, if you want me to. Monday, I'll let you know for sure."

He put his arms around her again.

"You'd better tell me good-by now, and go," she said, and stood up.

He stood up, too. There was so much he had to say, and nothing but words to say it with. And he couldn't even find the words to tell her something. Something that he knew was terribly important for both of them. And then it came to him.

"I love you," he said. "You knew that, didn't you?"

"Yes," she said, "I think I did. But thank you for telling me."

"I'll always love you," he repeated. It was no idle word he spoke. It was the light and the meaning and the purpose of life. It was eternal truth. He put his arms around her once more.

"And I you," she said. For a second they stood so, and then she moved gently in his arms.

"You'd better go now," she said.

He kissed her again and walked out into the dim, wet dusk. She stood in the door, watching him. The light behind her made a sort of golden circle, as if she were the focal point of all truth and beauty.

At the corner he turned to look back. She was still standing there, and something told him he must go back to her. That unless he did, he would never see her again.

But even as he hesitated, she closed the door, so that where there had been light before, now there was only an opaque rectangle of darkness.

Professor Elrod took off his glasses now, wiped them carefully and replaced them, and turned to Bill Gregory's paper as if in that single gesture, he was bringing himself back across the dozen or more years that lay between him and that closed door. He wondered now, as he had so often wondered, what would have happened had he gone back that evening as he had known he should: what would have happened if he had insisted on Amy's decision then. Or, perhaps, even made the decision himself, for both of them. Would that have prevented her from going to her cousin's, and so have saved her from the accident on the icy roads—the accident that cost her life?

That, of course, he could not know. For she did go, and the premonition he'd had as he looked at her there in the door had been right. He never saw her again.

No, that was not the way of it. He saw her every day. In everything he did, in every student he taught. For his head-wisdom in teaching might have come from Lois, but his heart-wisdom came from Amy. And it was his heart-wisdom he drew upon to meet the real problems of his students.

It would be his heart-wisdom that would speak to Bill Gregory now, telling him he must not ask perfection of this imperfect world, nor of himself, nor of the things that came to him. One cannot die inside himself because his dreams have died. There are still glories to be found, if one can only recognize them. There are still beautiful things left in the world—profound things, like the gold of an ash tree in fall; simple things, like the knowledge that there is more to life than the things one wants for oneself.

And, best of all perhaps, the realization that maybe it is only in imperfection that one can find the real meaning of life, since life, itself, is rooted in imperfection.

He picked up his papers, stacked them away in his desk. No need to check them before Bill came in for their conference. He closed the desk drawer, stood up by the window the better to see the ash tree by the fountain.

He thought that never before, in all the years he had been here, had he seen it quite this lovely.

The Halfway Tree

I WILL ALWAYS REMEMBER THAT SUMMER BECAUSE, AT ITS beginning, the fabric of my faith was still whole and unblemished. I was eight years old and for all I knew the great wide world was merely an extension of my own small one —a place filled with good and kind people who loved me and each other. How long this would have lasted I cannot say had not Cousin Mattie Lee Ford came up from Kentucky to visit her Missouri kin.

We went to Aunt Carrie's for dinner that Sunday, Papa and Mama and I, riding in a shiny new buggy which Mark, a high-stepping bay, pulled as easily as if we were no weight at all. Aunt Carrie was Papa's sister and the most satisfying kind of an aunt to have. She always said, just as soon as she hugged and kissed me, "My goodness, Janie, you do look more like your Mama every single day you live." This gave me a warm, comfortable feeling. Mama was the most beautiful woman I knew. If I looked like her, I would be pretty and everyone would love me, as they did Mama. That was all a woman needed to be, I thought happily—beautiful and charming. Growing up held only pleasant prospects for me.

"I suppose," Papa said, touching Mark lightly with the whip, "that Carrie will have the house full, as usual."

"Of course," Mama said, and the two of them exchanged a warm happy smile over my head but managing, at the same time, to make me feel I was a part of it, or perhaps even the reason for it.

From my place between them I looked first at one, then at the other. Even when Papa was sitting down you could tell he was tall. He wore a small, dark, closely cropped mustache. His hair was dark, too, and when he took off his hat (as he had done today, giving it to Mama to hold in her lap) there was a wave around his hair where the hat had rested. His eyes were dark, with small wrinkles at the corners, which came because he laughed a lot. I was sure Papa was the handsomest man in the world, and the gayest, and the best. I thought Mama looked especially lovely today in a muslin dress sprigged with violets, the color of her eyes. About her was the delicate scent of violets, the perfume which she always wore.

"Here's the halfway tree," I said, partly because looking at them made me so happy I had to say something and partly because I could never pass the tree without calling attention to it.

It was a huge cottonwood which Papa said was the oldest and largest tree in the county. It stood at the spot where the road crossed the creek, its branches hanging down to touch the edge of the bridge. I loved it because it was exactly halfway between our house and Aunt Carrie's so that, whichever way we went, I knew when we came to it that we were halfway to delight. Today Papa looked at it critically. "It's probably hollow inside," he said. "Some day it's going to fall and break the bridge down."

I was upset. The tree was mine, and I wanted no flaw in it. Mama was disturbed, but for a different reason. She said why didn't Papa—or someone—cut it down before that happened, and even as a protest crowded to my lips, Papa laughed lightly and said she wasn't to worry her pretty little head about it. The tree would probably stand another hundred years. He reached across me to pat her hand and she smiled back, so right away I felt better.

When we came to Aunt Carrie's, sure enough we saw that a lot of the kinfolks had already arrived. Papa's kinfolks, for Mama was an orphan who had come from Ohio to marry Papa and take his family and their ways for her own. Papa tied the horse, helped Mama out and lifted me to the ground. Then we walked to the door.

Aunt Carrie rushed to meet us, hugging and kissing us as if we had been separated for years. Aunt Hilda, Papa's other sister, came over to kiss us, too, although she lived next door to us and had seen us only this morning.

"Hello, everybody," Papa was saying when a woman came

toward him.

She was a little on the plump side with skin the color and texture of magnolia blossoms. Her strawberry blond hair had a high pompadour in front, and in the back one fat curl hung down, draping itself across her shoulder. In contrast to Mama, who was small and delicately made, she looked rather like an oversized rose just before its petals were ready to drop. She made straight for Papa, her arms outstretched.

"Why, Boyd Ferguson," she cried.

"Mattie Lee—" Papa said. He put his arms around her, swung her up off the floor, kissing her several times. Mama just stood there, watching. Finally Papa put Cousin Mattie Lee back on her feet and she stood regarding him, her head on one side, the fat curl sliding across her shoulder as she did so.

"I declare to goodness, Boyd Ferguson," she said, her voice seeming to come from way down in her throat, "you get bigger and better looking every day you live. How long has it been—ten years?"

Only she didn't say it quite that way. It was "declah" and "biggah" and "bettah."

"I guess ten years is about right," Papa agreed. He turned, reached toward Mama and pulled her to his side. "You haven't met my wife," he said. "Ruth, this is Cousin Mattie Lee Ford."

"How do you do," Mama said, holding out her hand. The woman looked at her, a sort of sizing-up look. Mama was accustomed to Papa's sisters looking at her, saying wasn't she beautiful, and things like that, but even I could see this appraisal was different. Mama flushed a little, but she stood her ground. "It's good to have you with us," she said calmly.

"I reckon you don't know you came between Boyd and me," Cousin Mattie Lee said. "I thought I had him for sure that summer, but when he came home, here you were and snatched him away. I've never forgiven you for it."

She laughed when she said it, a laughter in which the aunts joined. Papa looked at Mama out of the corner of his eye. She smiled a little.

"And this is Janie," Mama said, taking my hand and pulling me toward her.

"Hello," Cousin Mattie Lee said, turning her smile on me for just a moment. Then she looked at Papa again. "She's going to look like you, Boyd."

The statement made me vaguely uneasy. Not that looking like Papa wouldn't be all right, but nobody had ever said that before. He was a man; I was supposed to look like Mama, who was a beautiful woman. I stole a quick glance at the mirror to see what lack had come over me in the past week.

"Oh," Papa said, "there's a lot of Ruth in her."

He didn't say I was *exactly* like Mama; even the aunts

didn't mention it the way they always did. They just said, "Now you all go into the parlor and catch up on all the news while we put dinner on the table."

Papa and Cousin Mattie Lee walked off, talking at the same time, laughing a great deal. Mama watched them go, hesitated a moment, and then turned back to help Aunt Hilda and Aunt Carrie with the meal.

As far as Cousin Mattie Lee was concerned, there might have been no one else at the table but Papa. Almost every word she said was directed to him, and for the most part she talked about that summer he had spent in Kentucky. It was "Do you remember this?" and "Do you remember that?" Everyone laughed at the things she was recalling, although none of them except Papa could have possibly known what the jokes were because he had gone by himself on that Kentucky visit. Somewhere during the course of the meal I began to realize that Mama wasn't joining in the laughter at all. Papa must have seen this, too, for he stopped laughing and looked at her uneasily a time or two. But Cousin Mattie Lee didn't seem to notice any difference; she kept right on with her chant of "Do you remember's."

She didn't let up even when we went out to see Uncle Will's new horse, Prince, and the thing he called a runabout—a sort of topless buggy with rubber-tired wheels and a single seat with spokes for the back and sides and a velvet cushion in the seat. Cousin Mattie Lee said did Papa remember the time they went buggy riding and got lost. Papa flushed a little and everyone laughed again. All except Mama. She stood, quiet and composed, and held me by the hand.

Mama sat very straight in the buggy on the way home that evening, not smiling, her mouth a thin tight little line. Papa tried several times to start a conversation, with no luck. I sat between them, miserable and unhappy. Finally Papa cleared his throat.

"Ruth," he began.

Mama looked at him, across my head, and I caught the meaning of her glance. Whatever he had to say was to wait until they got home and I was in bed. Something was wrong between Papa and Mama, and my world had ceased to seem safe and beautiful. I went to bed, feeling more unhappy than I had since the day I broke my favorite doll.

Whatever it was must have got straightened out all right, for the next morning Mama looked very smiling and happy. She hummed softly as she went about her work, and looked prettier than ever.

When Papa came home for dinner he brought a letter

for Mama which he had picked up at the post office. The envelope bore a black border and Mama turned a little pale even before she opened it. She read the closely written pages, and then told us that the letter said a distant cousin had died back in Ohio and left Mama a small legacy. But the will also said that Mama was to come out to Ohio and see that the cousin's personal effects were distributed according to a set of written directions she had left.

Mama didn't want to go a bit, but there didn't seem any way out of doing it, so two days later Papa drove her and me over to Granbury, where Uncle Will and Aunt Carrie lived, so we could catch the train to Ohio. We got there all right, and immediately Mama started the business of sorting out the effects of Mrs. Mary Lawson, a cousin twice removed, according to her last wishes.

Mama worked hard, but even so it took a long time. Papa wrote us that he missed us something awful, and that Mama was to hurry and get the job done and come home. Finally one letter came that sounded even more insistent than the others had done, so Mama wrote to Papa and set a date for our return, telling him to meet us in Granbury. Then she worked so fast that she was through a good two days before the time she had set.

"We'll surprise Papa," she said, gleeful as a little girl. "We'll just walk in on him and surprise him. Goodness— it's almost a month since we left home."

The Halfway Tree

It was very hot that day when we got off the train at Granbury. Mama wiped the perspiration off her face, looked around half expectantly, although she couldn't have thought anyone would meet her, for no one knew we were arriving this soon. Al Miller, the livery stable man, took us to Aunt Carrie's in his hack, and we walked in on her and Uncle Will just as they were sitting down to supper.

You never saw such a lot of hugging and kissing as went on. It would have all been perfect had Papa only been there to share the happy confusion.

"My, my, is Boyd ever going to be happy," Aunt Carrie said.

"How is he?" Mama asked, her cheeks turning a little pink as she spoke.

"Oh, fine, fine," Uncle Will broke in. "But just about worn to a frazzle like all the rest of us. With Mattie Lee here, everybody's trying to entertain her. Run, run, run all the time. And in this heat—"

"Oh, so she's still here." There was a slight edge of formality in Mama's voice. "Where's she staying?"

"At Hilda's. She started there, and she says it's too much trouble to move her things, so she makes that her headquarters."

It seemed to me that things had worked out fine. I hadn't liked Cousin Mattie Lee very much and I didn't believe Mama had either. If she were staying with Aunt Hilda, who

lived next door to us, I was glad Mama and I had been out
of town during the visit.

Mama looked a little absent-minded during the meal,
and as soon as it was over she said, "Will, would you mind
letting me borrow your horse and buggy so Janie and I can
go home this evening?"

"Right now?" Uncle Will asked.

"Right now," Mama said.

They tried to argue her out of it, saying that it was late,
and she had seven miles to go, and it looked like rain, and
she ought to wait until morning and let Papa come for her.
Mama said it didn't look much like rain, but if it was going
to, that was all the more reason for going home immediately.

"Prince is pretty mettlesome, and you've never driven
him before," Uncle Will pointed out.

"Of course, if you don't want me to drive him—" Mama
said.

"Now you know I don't mind," Uncle Will protested.

"My heavens," Aunt Carrie broke in, "you've got no business starting out at this time of night, in an open run-about
with a rain coming up."

But there was no moving Mama. I knew what was in
her mind. She had said she was going to surprise Papa, and
she wasn't about to give up the idea. So it ended up with
Mama and me driving off in the run-about, its shiny wheels

flashing in the air, the rubber tires making scarcely a sound, Prince stepping high and smartly.

They were right about the rain. We hadn't gone more than two miles before it hit. First a few big drops and then, out of a great stillness the thunder rolled. Lightning shot across the sky, so intense I could see it playing over the harness on Prince's back. Then lightning and thunder came together, so close they both seemed to explode in the buggy at the same time. I screamed, grabbed at Mama's arm. Prince reared straight in the air. For one awful moment I thought he was going to fall backward into our laps. Mama jerked her arm free. "Hold tight," she said, "to the side of the seat—" And after that she had no more time for me. She was too busy trying to calm the horse, holding the lines taut but not too tight. "There, there—Prince—" she said. She continued to manipulate the lines, talking all the while. Finally after what seemed like a lifetime, but must have been no more than five minutes, she had the horse reasonably quiet and steady again. Then she turned to me.

"Janie," she said, breathing quickly, much as I did when I had been running, "you must not do that again—scream —or grab my arm—understand?"

"Yes—" I whispered thickly.

Just then another flash of lightning ripped open the sky.

In spite of Mama's warning, I screamed and threw myself upon her. Again, as before, Prince reared.

"Janie," Mama cried, her voice rising above the storm. *"Get down on the floor—and stay there—"*

I was ready to do her bidding. It was too much to ask of anyone—to sit straight up in the middle of the storm, tempting it to strike. Just then another flash of lightning played around us, illuminating Mama's face. It was as white as milk. And suddenly I knew. *Mama was scared, too.* She might have set her mind and heart into a pattern of courage, but she was scared. It wasn't very brave of me to lie cowering on the floor while Mama drove us through the storm. The least I could do was to sit beside her and make no more trouble for her.

"No—" I said stubbornly. "I'll stay here—with you—"

For just a moment she took her eyes off Prince to look at me steadily. Even in the darkness I could feel the intensity of her gaze.

"All right," she said. "But you must not scream—must not grab at me—no matter what happens. Understand—"

"Yes—" I said. And this time I meant it.

Now the rain started, a solid sheet of water making it almost impossible for us to see any distance ahead. By instinct, rather than by sight, I knew we were coming to the bridge and the halfway tree. Mama tensed slightly and I knew what she was thinking. In this darkness and the rain it would be easy to miss the bridge entirely. Fortunately at that moment a flash of lightning showed us we were on the road, safe enough. Then, above the howling of the wind, we heard another sound. Not thunder, but a sharp cracking as if the very core of the earth was breaking apart. In a single instant knowledge came to both of us. Papa had said the tree would break apart some day, and this was it.

The sound came again, sharper now and louder. For a moment Mama seemed trying to rein Prince in, to stop. Then resolution came to her.

"Janie," she cried. "Hold tight—"

She touched the whip to Prince. He sprang forward. Like the wind he went. Mama leaned forward, too, as if the very will of her would urge him on yet faster. The rain washed over us. I held tight to the little spokes that formed the back and sides of the run-about. The planks of the bridge thundered under the wheels. Just above us there was an awful crashing sound, as if doom itself was overtaking us. Then we were off the bridge, and not a second too soon, for behind us the halfway tree fell, the ends of it hitting the back of the run-about, even grazing us. Mama did not seem to be aware of it; she was too busy trying to stop Prince's headlong flight, for the falling of the tree had set him off in a frenzy of fright. Mama was sawing on the reins. The great pull showed on her hands—her arms were straight out, her feet braced against the floor as she leaned back to give more pull to the lines. Finally she had the horse under control.

"We'll be all right now," she said, her voice shaky but sure. "You were a fine brave girl, Janie. You helped me a lot."

Sweet as her praise was, I could not bring myself to answer her. The halfway tree was gone, and a part of my world had gone with it—something substantial and solid; something I had thought would last forever. Then a comforting thought came to me. I had sat by Mama, had not lain on the floor, giving up to my own terror. Mama had said I helped her by being brave. I felt grown-up, and pleased. It came to me that maybe it wasn't enough for a woman to be just sweet and pretty. She also had to be brave in time of danger. If she felt fear, she must cover it up for the sake of others.

I decided that, once we were home, I'd talk to Mama about this matter.

The worst of the storm was over by the time we got home, although the rain was still falling. I saw a light burning in the living room, knew that meant Papa was at home, and not yet gone to bed. The warmth and beauty of that light, the safety and comfort of it, reached out toward us so that it was all life's goodness and happiness—a sure, dependable thing to be approached with confidence and joy.

"Papa's here," Mama said. "And we're home. Thank God."

My heart echoed her words. Papa and Mama and I were going to be together again. I could almost persuade myself it didn't matter that the halfway tree was gone.

We got out of the buggy. Mama tied Prince to the hitch-rack. Together we walked toward the house. We were soaking wet, and Mama's hat had blown away, but that didn't matter at all. She threw open the door and we walked in.

And there in the lamplight we saw them, Papa and Cousin Mattie Lee.

They were in each other's arms. I had seen Papa hugging Cousin Mattie Lee, that Sunday at Aunt Carrie's, but this was different. Even I could realize that. Her face was lifted to his; the fat curl had slipped so that now it hung down her back instead of across her shoulder, where she had been so careful to keep it, the only other time I had seen her. But that was not the whole difference. Then Papa had acted boyish and gay, holding her in his arms. Now he seemed a stranger, with all the lines of his face set in a different pattern. There was no certain thing to tell me, but still I knew that he was being drawn to her, yet was trying to pull away, both at the same time. As if, maybe, he was a bird and that curl a snake which was charming him.

For what seemed like an eternity we stood there, nobody

speaking, nobody moving. Then they broke apart.

"Ruth—" Papa said. His voice didn't sound like Papa at all. And then again, "Ruth—"

Mama did not answer. The water was running off her clothes; it made a little pool at her feet. Her hair was hanging loose around her shoulders and it, too, was wet so that it clung to her small head. I wanted to cry out to Papa and tell him why she was soaking, why her hair was drenched and hanging wildly around her face. But I could say no word. I could only stand there and look at them, those grown-ups. Papa standing away from Mama, as if some great gulf divided them. Cousin Mattie Lee looking at him in a way I had never seen a woman look at a man before. Mama, her face set like stone in a mask of unbelief and hurt. It was as if some great evil were there before me, dimly understood but nonetheless visible and menacing. I began to sob. The sound of my wails broke the spell.

"Janie," Mama said, turning to me swiftly, away from those others, "Janie, you are soaked. You must get out of those wet things and into bed at once."

She hustled me out of the room.

I remember a great deal of confusion. Mama whisked me into a hot bath and then into my nightgown. It was all so fast I had not even stopped crying when I found myself in bed with the covers pulled up under my chin and the light out.

"Good-night," Mama said, and kissed me.

After she left I began to cry again. I could not stop. It was more than reaction from fright, from the sorrow I had known at seeing the halfway tree gone. It went beyond the shock of that awful moment of finding Papa and Cousin Mattie Lee together.

I was weeping for the beautiful world I had lost, one I knew I would never be able to regain.

I awoke to the consciousness of something happening, something I could not put into words. My mouth felt thick and dry. My first impulse was to call for Mama, for consolation and a drink of water. Then remembrance came to me, so that I knew I must not bother her. The water I could get for myself. I slipped out of bed, started toward the kitchen.

A light was burning in the living room; the door was partly open and through this opening I could see Mama and Papa. Cousin Mattie Lee was gone and at first I thought that now it would be all right for me to go in and join my parents as I used to do when I awakened to find them still up. Then I hesitated, feeling instinctively that I should not do this.

Mama had on a wrapper. I must have been sleeping for some time, for her hair seemed almost dry now. It was still hanging loose around her shoulders, making her look like

269

a young girl. But she also looked old—older than I had ever seen her. And more beautiful, in a strange sort of way.

Papa sat near her, looking much the way I did when I had been naughty and was craving forgiveness. He was staring at his hands which he opened and closed as they lay on his knees. Then he began to speak.

"And that's the way it was, Ruth—" he said. "Like I told you. That's all—I give you my word."

Mama did not answer. I looked at her. Something was gone from her face that had used to be there. I couldn't explain what it was, but even so, I knew she'd never look quite the same again. That, as long as she lived her face would bear a faint touch of sadness. Not just sadness alone, but a mingling of the things which had happened to her that night. The terror she had known driving Prince through the storm, pushing him across the bridge before the halfway tree fell; the memory of finding Cousin Mattie Lee and Papa standing together in our living room, locked in each other's arms. Always she would bear the special stamp of women who have known hurt, and risen above it.

I knew, too, although at the time I could not have put my knowledge into words, that unless Mama said the right thing now, Papa would never stand on his feet again, free and proud as he had used to be. I thought I couldn't bear it if she didn't answer him. Her silence was a gulf between them—my parents, whom I had never seen separated before. I was torn between them; it was as if there were two distinct parts to me. In some strange way I seemed to feel, at one and the same time, Mama's need to forgive Papa and his to receive that forgiveness. And I knew that, unless they were brought together, I could never be whole again. I wanted to call out to them—to tell them these things.

Then, slowly, slowly, as if every part of the motion was something Mama was thinking through deeply, she extended her hand toward Papa. He got up, with much of the old quick impetuousness about him. He came toward her. Then for a moment he hesitated.

"You do understand?" he asked. "And you forgive me?"

"Yes," Mama said. "I do. And now don't let's talk about it any more."

"Darling—" Papa said, and then Mama went into his arms.

I stood at the half-open door, watching them. I couldn't have moved had I wanted to. I don't know how long I stood there, feeling alone and left out. By and by Mama turned a little in Papa's arms, and then she saw me.

"Janie," she said, "what are you doing out of bed!"

Papa turned, too, still keeping his arm around Mama. "Come here," Mama said to me.

I stood still. Maybe Papa realized I needed his invitation, too, before I could come to them.

"You'll take your death of cold," Papa said. He smiled at me. Mama smiled, too. It was as if their smiles were one wave of love, reaching out to me.

"Come on in," Papa said.

He spoke in much the old way, but with a little difference, too. Maybe, I thought, he'll never forget tonight, either. It's something that will be with all of us, the rest of our lives.

"Well, come on," he said, holding out his hand to me.

I started across the floor, came to where they stood. Mama and Papa each took one of my hands. Together the three of us made our way to the sofa. We sat down, with me between them. Mama pulled a part of her wrapper across my knees. Papa reached out his arm across the back of the sofa, embracing both of us.

"How do you feel?" Mama asked me.

Warmth and happiness engulfed me. It didn't matter that I'd never be able to pass the place where the halfway tree had stood without feeling a thrust of sadness in my heart. It didn't matter that, like Mama, I'd always remember, a little bit, about Papa and Cousin Mattie Lee. We were together again, Mama and Papa and I. The whole foundation of my world rested on this fact. And someway I knew that, just as Mama had brought us safely through the storm, she had also worked out this other thing—this closeness of ours.

A bright flash of understanding came to me. I knew suddenly about this business of being a woman. It would be good if I could be beautiful, and even better if I had courage. But most of all I would need a loving and an understanding heart.

"I feel fine," I told them. "Just fine—"